GHOST HOUSE

Stories by
Sara Connell

Ghost House: Stories
Copyright © 2022 by Sara Connell

All rights reserved. No part of this publication may be reproduced, distributed, or transmitted in any form or by any means, including photocopying, recording or other electronic or mechanical methods, without the prior written permission of the author, except in the case of brief quotations embodied in reviews and certain other non-commercial uses permitted by copyright law.

This is a work of fiction. Any characters, businesses, places, events, and incidents are either the products of the author's imagination or used in a fictitious manner. Any resemblance to actual persons, living or dead, or actual events is purely coincidental.

Printed in the United States of America

ISBN 9781958714041 (Hardcover)
ISBN 9781958714034 (Paperback)
ISBN 9781958714058 (eBook)

Library of Congress Control Number: 2022942969

MUSE LITERARY

CHICAGO · NEW YORK · PARIS · ROME

Muse Literary
3319 N. Cicero Avenue
Chicago IL 60641-9998

CONTENTS

Introduction 9
Ghost House 11
Les Grenouilles 35
Terroir 47
Girls 61
Marionettes 67
Tarifa 79
Night Sky 83
Powell's Priests 97
One More 99
Salad 115
Unending Day 121
Not My Body 141
Acknowledgments 143
About the Author 145

To the spirits . . . thank you, all of you.

"One need not be a chamber to be haunted,
One need not be a house;
The brain has corridors surpassing
Material place."
—Emily Dickinson

"You don't seem too haunted, but you haunted."
—Terrance Hayes

INTRODUCTION

At Heather Kogut's birthday party in second grade, I told a basement full of girls in sleeping bags my dramatic rendition of the "The Golden Arm." By midnight, all eight girls had called their parents to come get them and I came a hair's width close to being banned from the slumber party circuit. I couldn't understand why they wanted to leave. Ouji boards, seances, magic eight balls, light as a feather, still as a board, the TIME life book series on ESP with covers bearing a gigantic purple eye- I grabbed at any whisps of the occult that my suburban childhood in Alexandria, Virginia afforded me. Other kids grew out of this phase, but I never did. Now, still, in my forties, (I am still friends with Heather by the way), I will eagerly buy any book with ghost in the title and have no shame and cracking open a deck of oracle cards when my friends come over for dinner. My delight and fascination with the spiritual realm has deepened as I took full on the task of healing a host of traumas that showed me how very many ways we as humans can actually be haunted.

It's been said by multiple writers that "every story is a ghost story." I agree. Some of the stories in this book contain ghosts, others arise from those other types of hauntings and my hope is that they will offer you something. A laugh, a micro healing perhaps and most of all I pray that they will take you back to a basement floor with sleeping bags fanned in a circle and a flashlight held up under your chin and a sliver shiver running happily up your spine.

GHOST HOUSE

"The thing about it is," Caitlin's husband whispered in her ear, "the sale of the Powell piece alone would cover the down payment. I could renovate this place and double our investment."

"Absolutely," the realtor, Ashley, said, eavesdropping. Ashley had blond hair with expensive highlights and wore navy ballet flats with a gold Tory Burch insignia on the toe. "Three bedrooms, en-suite master bath with dual sinks, original Tudor design. The ghost is part of the opportunity." Caitlin placed a dime on the floor. The coin rolled toward the closet and landed on the south side of the room. Were the warped floors also part of the opportunity?

"The thing about it is," Caitlin wanted to reply, "a ghost house is a terrible idea." John always told people what the thing about it was. When she started dating John, Caitlin thought this phrase was sweet, part of his unique snowflake, until their engagement party in Leatherstown, New York, where she found all the men in John's family started conversations this way. Now, every time John said it, she saw Buffalo Bills jerseys and rusted Chevelles up on cinder blocks and heard the slight K on the end of *thing*—the way John's uncles all said it.

Caitlin walked the perimeter of the room. Slanted floors, heavy oak doors. Stained glass windows. Nothing at all like the freshly built single-level houses with monochromatic kitchens and gallery white walls she wanted.

Ashley tapped the dark brown windowpane with a polished red fingernail. "Whoever takes this place will make a mint."

John announced that this bedroom would be the nursery and the realtor winked at Caitlin. There was a third bedroom too, which John had already claimed. "Built-ins," he said. He waved his hands in the direction of a floor-to-ceiling wall of dull, pealing walnut, bookcases that would house his collection of die-cut replica cars. Caitlin had lugged boxes of the cars up four flights of stairs when they'd moved into their condo. British racing green Aston Martins with nylon belts strapped across their engines; a pair of '65 Mustangs, Candy Apple Red; a '57 Chevy Bel Air, patent-leather black with shark fin tips sticking off the back; and John's favorite, a silver and blue '63 Corvette split-window coupe with snow-cap-white seats that John's father had given him and that had moved with him to every place he'd lived since childhood.

John pulled Caitlin's elbow and turned her toward Ashley, who was saying something about the closet. Was the ghost seething inside that door, waiting to unleash an eardrum-splitting screech?

"Does the ghost roam around?" Caitlin asked. When Caitlin tried to imagine the ghost, she could only conjure a white mist like from a children's cartoon. She hovered her hand over the knob.

"Attic," the realtor said and thumbed the air toward the ceiling. "According to the inspector, she never comes out."

Caitlin moved to the window. *She*. A female ghost. A blue jay the size of Caitlin's palm tapped on the glass pane of the bedroom window. The face was tiny and fierce, framed by a black mane. Caitlin watched its beak peck the glass.

The realtor walked them through the kitchen (brown everywhere, awful), the basement stuffed with exposed pink insulation pads and a yard of tangled weeds.

"This will be Caitlin's studio," John announced when they came to a large room on the first floor. The realtor looked at John with radiant admiration—this husband was so supportive of his successful artist wife.

The walls in this room were the same eggshell white of the Pemberton Gallery on her college campus; a lowly array of mostly bad student work. Even in the beginning, her work garnered some attention, though no money. John had hovered at the back of a group of professors and parents who spoke about her and her art as if she too were a sculpture adorning the room. "Such a bold young woman—like Louis Bourgeois and Brâncuși's love child."

John waited until there was a parting in the crowd before he approached. "What were you going for here?" He was the only person who'd ever asked her.

And everyone loved John. When they visited Caitlyn's grandmother to announce their engagement, John had walked around her nana's sizable backyard and asked her how she kept the rabbits out of the rose bushes. Nana bubbled about her floriculture tribulations while John nodded sympathetically and pulled the weeds he intuited had become a burden on Nana's knees and back.

Nana, Caitlin's mother, her studio mate in grad school, saw the same softness which he must have brought to the PE department of John Adams Elementary before the program lost funding and John was let go.

The job search wore at him. Rejection gave him indigestion and insomnia.

Nana said John was made to teach children, on weekends a gentleman farmer like the men in British magazines wearing wellies as they tended the rose bushes on their large estates. He was sensitive and tenderhearted. The only time she'd seen another side of him was on their honeymoon (a staycation was all they could afford). One night they splurged for dinner at a local vineyard. The chef served sea bream with hollandaise foam and giant fava beans rolled in butter. A drunk man at a nearby table mocked their waiter who was hearing impaired. John's face darkened and he watched until the drunk man rose to leave, tossed his napkin into the man's path, and then turned back to the beans while the man tripped over the soft linen and tumbled like an oak. The man broke a tooth and scraped an elbow badly enough to need a bandage. Someone had to have seen John throw the napkin, Caitlin was certain, but no one said a thing. When she recalled the incident later, she imagined that if someone had noticed, they'd felt the way she did. That the drunk guy was an asshole. Had it coming.

"This room is as big as our current condo," John said, rubbing his palms. "No more hauling marble up and down to the storage unit basement."

Caitlin's eyelid twitched, an anxiety symptom. She'd have this big studio and John would have the hundred-year-old pipes, old bathrooms, outdated kitchen—all for him to repair, John who'd never fixed so much as a toilet. In the midst of all of that, if John had his way, they would have a baby.

"Edward, Randall, Nythia . . ." John had listed all their friends to her last week. "All pregnant or have toddlers already," he said, as though procreation were a running race and they were behind. "You said you wanted this—big house, the kids."

Had she said it? She'd more *not* said she didn't want it.

"There are no other ghost homes on the market in the neighborhood," Ashley said. For weeks, this was all John had talked about. He'd place an open newspaper on top of her breakfast plate each morning. She reached for the coffee and sighed as she read about a ghost that had saved a two-year-old from drowning in the family's pool in New Jersey. Last week, an article stated that one of the Lauder heiresses moved into a ghost house on the Upper West Side of Manhattan. He added internet reports citing studies that showed ghosts helped extend the life of the elderly and Facebook ads that stressed the benefits of ghosts as free, constant companions for octogenarians, without the mess of pets.

Unless someone in the new homes died tragically and quickly, Caitlin and John's would be one of only two ghost houses in the area. The agent left them alone to talk.

"The thing about it is, we'd be fools not to take it," John said.

GHOST HOUSE

The ghost did not like Caitlin; she could tell right away. It waited until John left for Home Depot and Caitlin was sitting in front of a four-by-four slab of deep peach Tennessee marble for the Powell piece to knock over the bud vase on the kitchen table and pull each of the petals off the stalk.

The Powell project felt ill-fated. Mr. Lamott, the Powell's manager, insisted on an in-person studio visit with Caitlin in the condo before wiring the deposit. He wore a black suit and a pencil-thin black tie and had tiny teeth. Looked like he wouldn't mind killing a person with a baseball bat.

As if summoned by the image of Mr. Lamott, a sound came above Caitlin's head, like a body dropping to the floor. Caitlin gripped the end of the table and braced herself for the ceiling to crash onto her head. The metal shelves along the wall shook just a bit, like a train had rumbled by. The noise came over and over. *Thump. Thump. Thump.* Caitlin pictured the ghost lifting and smashing something—like a medicine ball with leather sections and white stitching.

She slumped into the velvet couch she'd moved over from the condo. Something was wrong with her work anyway. In the condo, with her work tumbling into their living room, her tools in a white bucket near the bookcase, she still felt like a college student—no pressure to create a perfect piece. She was unused to the press releases, commissioned assignments, gallery deadlines. For the past seven years, she'd taught art classes at the community college. Tended bar at the Brasserie two nights a week to make her half of the rent. Watching faces lengthen like Modigliani figures in the gold-gilded mirrors as she skewered olives onto sticks, the espresso machine hissing in the background. Her time in the Brasserie emptied her, left her open to talk to the stone the next day. The reality that her abstract figures of Persephone and Nyx and Asteria were selling now for $5,000, then $10,000, then $25,000 astonished and terrified her.

15

GHOST HOUSE

And now $60,000, for the Powells.

Caitlin circled the stone again. She'd been stuck making art only once before, during her senior year. After a slicing critique from a gallery owner who the professor had invited to view promising students' work, Caitlin tried on a life without art. For the first four days of her self-imposed exile, she'd gone to the gym, had lunch at Mod Pizza with friends, and participated in a ping pong tournament at a fraternity, figuring she might want to see what had been going on for these years while she spent every night at the artist studios. Quickly, she began to feel unwell. Her skin took on a gray tone and grew pimples. She was hungry but became bloated the minute she ate. She couldn't shit and spent a horribly embarrassing hour at student health while an intern walked her through a humiliating protocol to get unimpacted. The attempt failed. In desperation to move her bowels and eventually sleep, Caitlin slouched into the studio. All it took was fifteen minutes. She'd shivered over the bowl in the bathroom as two weeks of backlogged stool shot out of her asshole. She went home, slept for twelve hours, and when she woke up, the sun cutting lines through the bedspread, she dropped to her knees and said to the muse or whatever universal power was running this kind of thing, "I'm yours. I'll give you everything. I'll never quit again."

Up until the move into this big, drafty house, the steel point, her favorite chisel, had felt like a long, sixth finger. She'd hold the point against the side of a new piece of stone and the stone told her where to hammer and cut. Today, she'd walked around the marble for hours, stroking her palms over the dusky puce rock while the ghost banged that thing above her head. Now, her fingers felt like knobs.

She cooked peas and plain pasta with butter for dinner, like a child. John complained that she wouldn't even sit with him while he ate the filet he'd bought at the organic butcher he'd found on 26th Street.

"When you eat meat, the fear from the animal at the time it was killed transfers into your body," Caitlin said. She'd told John before that to create her art she needed to keep her energy light, her vibration high.

At nine, she lay alone on the bald mattress, too tired to pull the sheets from the dryer, while John watched TV downstairs. He'd already unpacked his free weights and their kitchen appliances. His model cars were dusted and positioned in order of value on the thick shelves in the extra bedroom.

When her eyes closed, she saw the stacks of boxes lining the walls of her studio, shaming her. Art books, rifflers, rasps, chisels, silicon wedges, anti-vibration gloves, sketch pads, and trays of charcoals that had likely broken in transit. She heard a laugh track and then the chimes from the introduction to a crime show. She'd done nothing all day yet she was exhausted.

All night, there was howling in the attic. Terrible, retching noises, like listening to someone vomit.

"I slept fine," John said the next morning. "I just tune it out."

Caitlin pressed an ice pack to the side of her head and walked across the street to the other ghost house on their block.

"Oh no, our ghost does nothing like that," the neighbor, whose name was Tonya, said when Caitlin told her about the thumping and howling. "We'd never live in a ghostless house again." She poured iced tea from a pitcher with lemons floating on top and handed the glass to Caitlin.

Tonya's ghost was respectful of the family—magnanimous, even. He patrolled the house at night, cleaned up messes, fluffed their pillows, and even arranged flowers in a vase if they laid some out on the counter.

"He helped blow out the candles at Amina's birthday party last year."

Caitlin watched Tonya's children climb up the beams of a wooden playhouse in the backyard. "Why do only some ghosts remain in a house?" she asked. "People die at home all the time."

Tonya's eyes brightened. "There's so much to learn when you get a ghost. For instance, if the ghost attaches to a house, the people they left behind can visit one day a year," she said. "Everyone expects visiting day to be Halloween—or November 1. But it's May 15."

Twelve people from Tonya's ghost's family had shown up the previous May. "I didn't see anybody visit your ghost, though," Tonya said. "So sad for her."

John came home the next day with flowers wrapped in brown paper and cellophane: pumpkin-orange petals, stamens covered in pollen. "To inspire you," he said. Caitlin locked her jaw and reached in the back of their cabinets for a larger vase. The ghost waited for them to go to sleep, then shredded the flowers in the garbage disposal. While Caitlin visited Tonya, the ghost had dumped her sketchbook in the bathroom sink and left the water running. Caitlin had blown each page dry with a hair dryer, but the pencil had blurred into the paper so she could no longer see any individual lines.

Her phone pinged. Mr. Lamott, the Powell's house manager, requested an update. She began to compose a text and stopped. He'd given her four weeks; only two remained. She turned her phone face down on the glass table John had purchased from a consignment shop. The piece must be at least three feet high, Mr. Lamott had said. To grace the foyer of the Powell's new Greenwich house. Caitlin pushed the marble out of the studio and into the living room on a dolly and tried to recreate the atmosphere of the condo, with its cramped furniture and clean white light spilling onto the carpet. The light was yellow and clouded the lead-lined windows. The stone refused to speak. She'd forced herself to make at least one cut before John returned to the left side of the stone and instantly regretted it. The hole gaped like a pulled tooth.

The ghost moved over the living room ceiling, right where Caitlin sat, and began to drop the medicine ball above her head.

"I can't take it," Caitlin said when John returned from a workshop on plumbing.

"The thing about it is," John said, "the house is getting more valuable by the day."

He handed her a glossy magazine he'd plucked from the rack at the grocery store. A Cambridge study showed large quantities of dark matter passed through the human body weekly and were now thought to be the cause of seven strains of the most common cancers, as well as dementia and Parkinson's disease. Ghosts, being transparent themselves and unable to radiate, absorbed 80 percent of the dark matter in a home. Like a cosmic air purifier, they could help humans live an average of ten additional years.

A *decade more with your loved ones* was now a slogan on real estate billboards. Ghost houses were selling before they were on the market for tens of thousands above the asking price. Longer life and a million dollars if they stayed even one year, John reasoned. Surely replacing a sketchpad and putting up with some noise in exchange for all this prosperity was worth it.

"I'm much more interested in what's going on in *here* than in the ghost anyway," John said, squeezing Caitlin's thigh. He showed her an app he'd downloaded that would chime when she was ovulating.

Caitlin's mind jumped to the bare pre-nursery room upstairs. Was a person allowed to say yes to something and later change her mind? Caitlin assumed when they'd gotten a bit further into the marriage, the desire would've kicked in. She'd never been anti-child but she'd also not understood what the art would ask of her.

She'd watched a documentary once. The camera followed a group of fine artists, mostly painters, who were a stretched and haggard lot that carried the energy of stray dogs scavenging for food. They worked in the middle of the night after the kids were asleep, some set alarms before dawn to go to work, and one who had a minuscule apartment in Manhattan wrote sitting on the toilet from 4:00–6:00 every morning while the rest of the family slept. Caitlin read that Shirley Jackson managed to both care for her four children and crank out her books by taking speed, which then gave her a heart attack. Motherhood actually killed her.

Caitlin knew these thoughts were hyperbolic. People hired babysitters or nannies. The women in the doc weren't women of means. They'd had to do it all themselves and they'd suffered for it. Selfish was the word John would use, that Caitlin's mother would use. She was selfish. For time, for space, for quiet, for the soft-brain limbic space that she was now free to indulge in daily and from which all the art came. She had never been a command performer. Her artistic vision rose out of that waking dream state, the aimless walking past the sycamore trees in the park and the crunch of leaves under the rubber soles of her shoes. She feared the muse that had claimed Caitlin would not share her.

But none of this would matter to John. He'd deny the reality that her art commissions now paid for their life and if they went away, they'd have nothing. She'd said "I do" to John and his dream of a family. John's chance to do over his childhood. She saw John's battle wounds every day. The crumpling of his face when he saw a small boy holding his mother's hand at the park. Ovarian cancer with his mother, basal blastoma for his father, a college friend smashed by a drunk driver. He bore it like a curse. Caitlin's great-grandmother had lived until ninety-eight. John picked her for her good genes. In John's sequel, no one died. Everyone stayed.

Caitlin imagined herself wrestling a stroller down the stairs while a ghost flew around and in front of her, blocking her way, flinging cartons of formula onto the floor. Everyone said marriage ruined sex, but she worried deeply that motherhood killed art. All the insatiable giving of oneself, one's time, creativity. She could see out a few months into the baby's infancy, her energy draining and bleeding out.

Caitlin excused herself, walked past the bathroom, and into the cold diesel plume of the garage. She reached for a foil packet in the glove compartment of her Buick, swallowed a blue pill as small as a comma, and went inside to make love with John.

"Maybe we should see an endocrinologist," John said. "We could afford it now. Sunish and Nythia had twins with IVF."

His eyes lit. Twins would be even better than one child, he said. One pregnancy, two children. If she kept taking commissions, they could afford private school. Such abundance.

That night, the ghost wailed from 5:00 to 8:00 a.m. When she finally dragged herself out of bed, she walked into the nightstand and watched as a purple bruise spidered across her thigh.

"The thing about it is, we can fix this. I'll pick you up some noise-canceling headphones," John said when he left on his errands. Later, he was going to nail up Smartwall to finish the basement; the salesperson at Lowes had told him was easy to install.

Caitlin stared at the marble lump. The piece was now a four-foot-tall slab with stumps for arms and a misshapen head. Mr. Lamott had left two more messages and asked for a photo to demonstrate her progress. Caitlin had let the phone battery leak until the screen went black.

Outside the window, she saw a white van pull up at Tonya's house. A large insect—black, with pincers and beetle eyes—covered the flat-paneled side of the van. The driver wore a gray jumpsuit and carried a canister with a black hose. Caitlin waited until he came back out of Tonya's house before she accosted him.

"Do your chemicals work on non-living things?"

The man spun toward Caitlin's house. "I see somethin'," he said. "Up there." He pointed to the attic.

Caitlin pulled her elbows close to her ribs. Could the ghost hear her across the street? She thought she heard something crashing down the stairs. She dropped her voice and whispered urgently, "Can you remove other entities? Poltergeists? Phantasms? You know—" She moved her head back and forth as if shaking snow off her shoulders. "Ghosts?"

The man spit a piece of pink gum into a wrapper. "I get rid of bugs," he said. "I could check your walls for termites."

In Caitlin's absence, to punish her inquiry, the ghost had taken on the kitchen—upturned every cereal box in the pantry onto the floor, making a carpet of oats and flax seed, and unhinged the side kitchen door. The door gap left a hole like a train tunnel. A flock of squirrels, blue jays, finches, and a robin had invaded and shat on the new gray slate.

It took Caitlin two hours to clean. She would never get the bird nail scratch marks off the slate. She should have left the mess for John, but she needed an excuse not to work.

Before the move, she had suffered only from too many ideas: shapes and statues had peeked out from behind bushes, in the doorway of the brasserie, in the air in front of her eyes. Now, cut off from inspiration, she brought back old, superstitious behaviors from childhood—walking sideways through doors, stepping over cracks in the pavements, and still found only a blank, empty space inside her brain. Cohabitating with the ghost had muted her.

Caitlin searched online and found an obituary for her house address in the *Oban Sentinel*.

Mary Ann Sinclair, forty-six. Died from blunt force trauma to the brain.

An intruder had left a size twelve footprint on the hardwood floor of the bedroom before leaping from the second-story window of the bedroom. He was never found. Mary Ann's husband, Samuel, and daughter, Anna Lee (eleven), had been in the next town at a basketball game.

Caitlin climbed the steps to the attic door. The wood was so old it was almost blue—like an illustration of attic stairs in a book instead of real stairs.

She heard nothing behind the thin door.

"Maybe I can help find your family," Caitlin said—loudly enough, she hoped, to be heard through the wood. She told the ghost about the visitor's day. "It's something about the veil between the living and spirit world being thin at that time. I could locate your husband and daughter. Bring them here?"

The attic possessed a stillness so complete that she could hear, in contrast, the sound of a woodpecker in the large oak in front of the house. Caitlin pressed her hands against the wood, which was warm. She felt a wave of humidity that reminded her of standing on a dock in South Florida, a salty place her parents took her once on a vacation where she could go nowhere without sand blowing into the creases of her elbows and inside her underwear. She stood thinking about that place—the swordfish pulled out of the sea on bloody hooks and then cooked up on coals brushed with rosemary sprigs.

The attic door in front of her chest splintered as if a foot had kicked through the planks. She could see no foot, just the effect of a foot: the smell of sawdust, fractured wood. Caitlin ran. Her scream lodged in the muscles of her throat.

"We have to move," Caitlin said.

"I'll fix the attic door," John said. "The thing about it is, I just need six more months to flip the house. I supported you all those years before you sold anything."

Caitlin's longing for that time came like a hunger. Spacious, empty afternoons, the only sounds the grinder and etching hammer cracking against marble. John arriving home from teaching PE to bands of beloved and sweaty students.

———————

Phantomology was a burgeoning field. Duke's Rhine Center had been open for years, but Harvard offered a master's program now, and Amherst, Stanford, and UCLA had followed. Caitlin took her laptop into the bathroom and filled out a form and paid ninety-seven dollars online.

The report from Dr. Moore at Southern Cal arrived in her inbox the following morning.

The only way to remove the ghost is to do a scourge. The spirit disintegrates into sub-matter and is sucked through a tube into a container that would be disposed of via satellite. The process is unpleasant. The ghost is pulled apart bit by bit. We believe they feel the kind of pain a living person would feel. We don't know if the disintegration process alters anything at the level of the soul. We're not disposing of a body here; we're working at the level beyond somatic. Because of this, we recommend trying every possible way to cohabitate harmoniously.

Caitlin felt fear thump in her kidneys. She had no interest in this type of responsibility. The ghost was already dead and now, if she did this scourge, Caitlin would be the agent of an action worse than killing: interfering with the immortality of a soul.

A loud stomp in the attic. Plaster from the ceiling fell like snow. A chunk of plaster hit the keyboard and sprayed into Caitlin's face. Caitlin's eyes stung. Her lungs filled up with dust. She ran from the room, leaving the computer to be buried in the ash.

"The thing about it is, a scourge will ruin the investment," John said, hurt that she'd ordered the report from Dr. Moore.

"If I don't finish this commission, we won't pay our mortgage."

John sulked and loudly rearranged his tools on his tool belt. Caitlin wondered if he'd looked up Mary Ann's obituary too. Mary Ann had been attractive before she died. The kind of olive skin and green eyes of both of the women John dated before Caitlin. A woman from Montana had been on TV last week describing an erotic encounter she'd had with the ghost who lived in her house. Maybe John wanted to fuck Mary Ann.

"Even with just another four months, we'll make six figures on the sale," John said. His phone beeped like a train. "Ovulating!" the message said in pink letters. When he shook the phone, confetti rained across the screen.

They made love, mechanical and dull at first. Then John's face went all blurry. Caitlin imagined she was fucking the termite exterminator, with his chemical-stained, nuclear hands scratching her skin. She came hard. After, she went to the garage and swallowed her pill.

The Powells' lawyer sent an email the next morning. We expect delivery on time in seven days per the legal agreement you've signed to this effect.

"Four months," John said. "In four months, we can put the house on the market."

He slid a sandwich and an orange into a paper bag before he left for a kitchen and bath seminar at a hotel near the airport, thirty miles away. "I'll be home late."

Caitlin waited until his car turned off their street. She pulled a pair of gardening gloves over her hands and chose the large sculpting mallet from her workroom. She slung safety goggles over her eyes. She held the point, her stone finger, hard enough to crack rock.

She surveyed the bookshelves in the study. John displayed his cars in order of financial value. The red Corvette in first place. It was worth more than two thousand on eBay, he'd bragged to a neighbor whom he'd brought over to see the cars.

Caitlin laid the tip of the Point on the rosy hood of the engine. Holding her breath, she brought the mallet to the back of the stem. The metal crunched nicely; the Point punctured the hood like a stake through a vampire heart. If a miniature person had been driving the car, they would have been impaled. She placed the car on the floor and slammed the mallet across its body. In under sixty seconds, the car lay like a corpse.

She took the cars one by one and shattered their chrome wings, flicked off their fenders, and cut the fins from the chassis. She crushed the windshields with the toe of her boot. She felt exhilarated and didn't want to stop. Caitlin checked her phone. She had time. She ran to the garage, got the blowtorch, and burned the Chevyl, the first car John's father bought him, until the seats were charred and the air smelled like ash.

She felt the air to see if she could sense Mary Ann in the room.

"Do you like to watch—or do you just like doing the destroying?" Caitlin yelled.

The floor was littered with busted-up fenders and hoods and wheels, a miniature apocalypse. She thought about which would be more disturbing for John: leaving the whole office full of metal chips and the carcasses of his cars, or lining them back up on the shelves, mangled and burned?

John made a sound like a dying bird when he saw the cars.

"We have to move," Caitlin said. "She'll destroy every good thing we have."

John held the charred hood of the Corvette to his heart and lay down with his chest pressed into his knees. Caitlin opened the windows. She turned a fan against the shreds of metal to see if she could steer the smell back out into the night. She wondered if she'd moved too quickly. Maybe John would have conceded the house if she'd just destroyed one car.

John refused to leave the room. Caitlin felt guilty and aroused. Maybe this was what Mary Ann wanted. To teach Caitlin the power of destruction to make her feel alive. Caitlin's fingers buzzed like she'd shocked herself on a light switch. She'd seen something begin to move between the spray of metal chips and model paint. Something quick and darting, like the silver flash of the side of a fish. A shape, a series of shapes. The Powell piece. She knew how to finish it.

She walked John to the bedroom, got him some water, and propped him up with all the down pillows. She laid a cool washcloth over his forehead and hummed something like a lullaby by Chopin. She stroked his hair until his eyes breath deepened and his eyes moved under his lids.

Once he was out, Caitlin dragged every plug-in light they owned into the studio. Three floor lamps and two halogen spots from the garage. She threw the Point and the mallet in a bucket. She dragged the thick marble back into the workroom and pushed it against the wall. Peach, pink, creamy white—the palette was too weak. She needed something different. She walked around her other slabs of marble, which stood unmoving like gravestones. She'd use the largest piece she had, a ten-foot slab of jet gray marble, almost black. She'd use only the pneumatics—the big tools.

The compression pen hissed and spat as it blew sections of marble into dust. In twelve hours, the piece was finished. The entire body created out of geometric shapes, rhombuses, circles, ovals, and squares hanging in perfect tension with each other.

The next morning, Caitlin felt the sensation before she was fully awake: a soreness in her breasts, a feeling of the ground shifting under her as if she were on a ship. The top of her head itched. It took a minute to place the sensation. A child waking her mother up in the night. *Mommy, I have to—*

Caitlin threw up, clutching the side of the sink.

She watched as John forced himself out of bed and met the Smartwall delivery van while still wearing his pajamas. His skin was green in tone, the light dim behind his eyes, as though his father had died all over again.

Caitlin's dizziness broke at ten. Her mouth watered. She ate a sleeve of bacon, beef jerky, the remnants of the lamb chop John had cooked for himself on Saturday. All these years avoiding this food when what she needed was iron, platelets, sinew, and bone. Had Mary Ann loved meat? Had she broken and crushed any of her husband's things when she was still alive? Caitlin left the dishes, the brown sauce from the meat like dried blood on the plate, in the sink. She wiped her mouth, prowled into the workroom, gripped the compression pen, and held the black marble like a lover.

"Pick up any time," she texted Mr. Lamott.

At three o'clock she vomited all the meat back up. She felt too dizzy to drive and walked the ten blocks to the pharmacy. She remembered her high school health teacher, a former wrestler with cauliflower ears and eyes that receded back into the flesh of his cheeks. "The Pill," he'd read to them from a pamphlet. "Only 99 percent effective."

She used the restroom at the gas station next to the drug store. Cold toilet. Grease smears on the mirror. Her urine hot as steam. Two pink lines on a white stick.

The next morning, Caitlin threw a sheet over the Powell piece. She had promised herself to stand guard until Mr. Lamott sent his van for the sculpture at a time to be determined by text. She imagined the ghost caterwauling into the studio, raising the saw above its invisible head, and splitting the piece in two.

Caitlin sat at the table, moving her hands across her belly. She could not stop giggling.

She called Tonya and asked if she wanted to send the girls over—get out and do some errands or something. Inside her living room, Caitlin braided the girls' hair. Amina and Lakisha, they politely told her their names. Gorgeous little girls with hair like spun caramel with gold flecks in their irises. She had never really looked at Tonya's children. Were all children so beautiful?

Caitlin found a bin of her old art supplies: broken crayons, markers with dry tips, a tub of clay almost too dry to use. She moistened the clay with drops of water from the faucet and set up objects on the table—showed them how to make the shape without taking their eyes off the scene before them, to mold the clay without looking at their hands. An anatomy doll, a vase of flowers, clementines rolling off the table.

"Magic!" Lakisha squealed.

Caitlin had never thought she wanted this. That she would feel such joy.

When they left, she threw the lights back on in the workroom and pulled the sheet from the Powell piece. How had she not thought of it before? To reduce the body to pure geometric form?

The baby, she decided, was helping her.

Mr. Lamott sent a text message that the men would be there to pick up the sculpture the following afternoon at four. It was only then, with the floor spot glaring down on the oval, serrated head, that Caitlin recognized the quiet running through the house. When was the last time she'd heard a *thwack* or a *thump*? Not since they moved in had the ghost allowed such stillness. The absence of sound unnerved her. She'd read dogs could smell when a woman was pregnant. Could ghosts also detect increases in estrogen, progesterone? Caitlin gripped the silver edge of the sculpting stepladder next to her.

Caitlin imagined herself wrestling a stroller down the stairs, her belly round as a beach ball; a warm puff of air behind her neck and then with no way to stop, her body in flight. After, blood clotting between her legs, a dark stain the shape of a lake on the floorboards.

The ghost would take it. Her sculpture, her baby, everything that brought her joy. Caitlin tried to pull the guest room mattress into the hallway. She would set up a room in the studio. No stairs until she and John moved out of this house. The mattress was unwieldy.

Her forearms started to sweat. Pregnant women weren't supposed to lift anything heavy—she'd read that somewhere, too.

Tonya was happy to refer a handyman. James arrived in work boots and the same tool belt John now hung over his waist every day. James dragged the mattress into the studio. Caitlin added a pillow and a throw from the living room.

"The ghost will ruin the sculpture," Caitlin told John when he glared at the mattress on the floor. "I have to guard it."

"The thing about it is, you are getting more insane every day," he said.

"We're all crazy," she said. She faked a laugh. As though she'd made a joke. She was no longer sure about either of them. Looking at the Powell commission that morning she had the feeling that the ghost was hovering above her, guiding, assisting.

She'd tell him about the baby—about the real reason she wouldn't go near the stairs—tomorrow. Or maybe in a few days. After she went to the doctor and took an official test. Just not quite yet.

Caitlin's not sure where she is in space. The air is pink and opal, like the inside of a seashell. The last thing she remembers is sandpaper in her hand. One little rough spot to polish down. A whoosh of air, her foot slipping off the shiny metal.

Her head hurts, her belly, too. Her belly! Her hand moves slowly, as if in water but she feels the round bump. Bigger now! How long was she asleep? But yes, still pregnant. The ghost obviously has done something. Changed frequencies, isn't that what Tonya said they could do? Threw some kind of energetic veil over the house.

Caitlin hears nothing. In fact, her ears are plugged. She reaches up but can't find her ears.

Mary Anne! She calls but no sound comes out. It's just a dream, silly.

She can fly in this dream. It's fun. Her pink dress caresses the baby and tickles her armpits. She's so pregnant she feels the baby's head pressing down on her cervix. She can see through floors and walls. She sees John moving downstairs in the house. Walking into her studio. He pulls the curtain back from Hera. That's what Caitlin named her. Zeus' strong, proud wife. He flicks the tarpaulin back in place. Not impressed, she guesses, but he never understood art. For a blink, she can see inside his head—like a movie. He sees her on the cover of *Art America*. Smiling next to Hera in the Sotheby's catalog. The images in his brain are gone then, but Caitlin feels a quickening through her ribs. She sees it, too.

Something extraordinary is going to happen for them. She will tell John about the baby and how she understands they can make it work. She'll get more commissions. He can take care of the baby while she works. They can clean up the yard, put in a pool next summer.

He's bending toward something now. The white bucket, where she keeps her tools for cleaning. He's scraping something off the bottom of the chisel. Candy apple red. British racing green. *I didn't mean it*, Caitlin tries to shout. It was the ghost—I wasn't myself. He doesn't even look upset. He's speaking but she can't hear him. She imagines the words. *The thing about it is, Caitlin,* I forgive you.

He pulls a screwdriver out of his pocket. He is so kind, tightening up the screws on her ladder. Looking out for her safety. She watches the yellow Phillips head spin in his hands like a prism.

It's a different day now, further into spring. Hydrangea and azalea bushes hum with bees. A pretty young realtor in a navy shift dress walks a couple up to a house across the street. "It's an A-frame, three-bedroom, four-bath, under a million," the pretty realtor tells the wife. "Nice, but I wish I could get you that one." She points right up to the window where Caitlin is hovering. "The wife was a sculptor. Her husband found her. She fell off a ladder and cracked her head on the corner of the table. Brain hemorrhage. The *Times* ran a piece—maybe you saw it."

The agent dropped her voice for this part. The graphic details of a ghost house were now often the tipping point to make a sale. The couple moved closer until they were almost touching her bright pink lips. "She was pregnant, you see. He didn't know."

The young couple's eyes widened.

"A three-ghost house." The agent sighed.

LES GRENOUILLES

The French teacher was fired on Monday. We assumed she must have sold drugs or tried to sleep with a student. If she did try to sleep with a student, we were jealous it hadn't been one of us, even the girls. Madame Camille was tall and young and had polished red nails and a long, black braid that fell over her shoulder and down her left breast. We did not know where her beauty had been forged. Cyprus, Ecuador, the Caribbean were all popular guesses. She wore gold sequined sneakers and had freckles on the bridge of her nose, eyes that were somewhere between turquoise and hazel green. She looked like the prediction photos of what humans will look like in the future when all our races merge and we stop hating each other.

"*Attendez!*" she would sing at the beginning of each class. Then, instead of having us fill out worksheets of the French name for things that go in the kitchen—*couteau, coullier, un plat*—Madame Camille would read our fortunes from a deck of tarot cards. Other days, she'd lead us into states of hypnosis using a finger-snapping technique, or read metaphysical texts about tapping into a universal mind, asserting that in this way, we'd simply "remember" French, not have to learn it. Sometimes, she'd play Sophie Alour and Airelle Besson from portable speakers and put a still life of a tall vase and a few lopsided oranges (*les oranges*) over a linen cloth on her desk (*bureau*).

"*Dessinez*," (draw) she instructed us, even though hers wasn't an art class. She'd walk between our desks and stop if we hesitated, her braid grazing our biceps, her hand covering our small fingers.

"*Regardez*," she'd say. "*Ce que vous voyez.*" Draw what you see. And even though we had always been miserable artists, our pastels would begin to fly across the page. The vase, *les oranges*, *le bureau* would appear as if we were possessed by Matisse and our drawings would be hung in the school hallways on days when the school gave tours.

On Tuesday, the principal announced that Madame Camille was let go for stealing one of the dissection frogs from the biology classroom. "I wanted you to hear it from me so you don't go spreading rumors," he said during morning announcements.

At six o'clock the previous Saturday evening, Madame Camille had been caught on the school's security cameras. She was a grainy vision of grace, walking smoothly in a pair of snakeskin boots into the classroom and bending over into the refrigerator where Mr. Haney had been storing twelve shrink-wrapped frogs in formaldehyde for the anatomy module.

Speculations sparked. "Madame Camille was selling them to the private girls' academy in Clinton because teacher pay was so poor." "She has some kind of sex fetish." "Madame Camille is in a cult and the frog was part of ritual sacrifice." "Madame Grenouilles! Madame Grenouilles!" How the few students who studied enough French to have learned the word "frog" began to refer to her.

The cult ritual theory captured our minds like a fever. "Weren't there cults in South America, or Mexico, where people drank frog blood?" we whispered to each other in the hallways.

We were a half-dozen Catholic girls and had been told by our mothers since birth that pagan rituals were satanic and would send us straight to hell. Our grandmothers told us stories, before arthritis, Parkinson's, dementia took them. Things about our ancestors who lived somewhere in the belly of France and helped people who couldn't walk or see or have babies to do these things. Our mothers straightened their hair and wore boxy suits and bought cheap shoes at TJ Maxx and talked nothing of our ancestors, except that they had all been good Catholics. "Ignore your grandmother's ravings," they'd say as they prodded our feet with broom handles to get us out of bed for mass on Sunday mornings.

Our mothers were happy no women stood behind the altars on Sunday or heard confessions on Thursdays in the dusty afternoon light of the sacristy. Mary was the vessel. Empty, chaste, visible only to put Christ, the leader, the power, in relief. This was no loss to us. We had no inclinations for priesthood or pulpit. We had problems no priest would be able to solve.

There was something wrong with our neural pathways. On certain days we couldn't write papers of conjugate verbs or diagram the phases of photosynthesis on a worksheet. Some of us tapped our feet or bounced pencils on our knees until our teachers threw us out of class. They used to give kids like us Ritalin and Adderall, but we didn't have ADHD. They didn't know what to call what ailed us. We walked around school with purple moon bruises under our eyes and blinked all the time and people moved away when they saw us coming down the hallway. Except Madame Camille.

"*Mes petites déesses*! My little goddesses," she'd say then hug us and kiss our foreheads, sneak us marzipan shaped like lemons and tiny birds. We circled her gratefully, greedily, radiating in her presence like explorers at the earth's poles in the dark months when they rarely saw the sun.

"The six short hairy freaks!" the eighth-grade girls would squawk and throw tampons at us in the hallway. Jaqueline had started her period at nine. All of us menstruated by ten. We grew coarse, curly dark hair across our pubic bones before we were out of third grade. Marie developed a limp. Our knuckles swelled at the change of each season. We found our files in the nurse's office. We had something, doctors speculated, caused by the milk we drank as toddlers or some fluorocarbons that came through the porous ozone layers. Super-sized cow hormones to keep a four-hundred-pound cow fertile enough to produce milk and calves and years longer than nature intended. They were now pumping through our kidneys, making our girl bodies into women while we were still collecting glitter stickers and reading *The Baby-Sitters Club*.

Our mothers took us to doctors, to endocrinologists, to radiologists. They measured our ulnas and marked them in a chart to be completed again in six months. They stuck our fingers and ferned droplets of our blood on glass slide plates to test our estrogen levels. They pulled our pants down or hiked up our shirts and took pictures of the curly hairs, like zoo animals. Our mothers smiled and said we were still God's children, but they looked at us differently after that—with repulsion, with fear, like we'd done something to bring on these fuller baby breasts, the simian hair.

The doctors said some of us would lose half a foot of height since menstruation came on too soon. Fertility issues, truncated life span—no one knew. Short of shooting us full of Triptodur, which had the unfortunate side effect of sterility and manic episodes, there was nothing they could do.

The big worry was Marie. She hadn't grown an inch since last March and the limp had crawled up her leg so that she used crutches most days. If her symptoms worsened, she'd be put in a chair. We heard our mothers at night sighing into their phones. A surgeon from St. Stephen's told Marie's mother that if her neurological issues, her limp, the tapping, did not improve in the next month, he would perform surgery. That meant putting a long needle through the flesh of her brain into her pituitary gland. Best case, her body would stop producing so much estrogen and she'd be calm, she'd walk. Worst case—well, that's when our mothers stopped talking and left us to twist in our beds and wake to their red eyes and balled-up Kleenex on the carpet.

By the week before Madame Camille was fired, we'd developed night terrors, lost our appetites, threw away the peanut butter and honey sandwiches our mothers handed us in the morning.

"Look," Marie called in the hallway after French class. The fear had vanished from her eyes. Color raged in her cheeks. She held a small box, let us stroke the purple leather cover. "It was a gift from Madame Camille."

"*Pour mes petites saints*," Madame Camille had written on a white note card stuck inside the front cover.

Inside, sepia-toned girls younger than us were levitating, backs arched in postures of rapture, bilocating themselves into other dimensions. The reverse side of each card described each girl as a saint's miracle. The theme for many of them: *spontaneous healings*.

"Those girls were just regular girls like us. They called on a divine power and it came through them. They made their own magic," Marie said. Dust particles hung in the sunlight around her face, giving her the appearance of a dandelion about to be blown away.

"We don't have any powers. All this happened centuries ago," we said.

Marie typed "modern saints" into Google. "See? Miracles being performed just this year by John of Padre in South America."

"We don't have money to fly to Brazil," we said.

We found Madame Camille's address easily enough on Google. She would tell us about the frogs, how to use them to perform a miracle. After school we took the 121 bus. It was spring and only another three weeks before summer and when the doctors would swallow Marie. Our sneakers left yellow pollen imprints on the sidewalk. The house was made of small red brick and cheap wood, built in the '50s like a lot of homes in our town. Two azalea bushes, ripe with fat yellow blossoms, flanked the front door. We could see the tiny sawing legs of at least three bees as we walked to the door. No answer. We crept around the back. We'd hoped to find a circle of vibrating women. Nothing like our mothers with their boxy suits and pinched faces. No, we imagined radiant women in peasant skirts and spider jewelry sitting along a five-pointed star drawn in chalk on the grass. Advice delivered to us in hushed tones when the sky turned indigo. The smell of palo santo sticks with smoking red tips stuck into the grass. A laying on of hands.

A dog barked. Backyard empty. We peaked, on tiptoe, into the window of Madame Camille's kitchen. Eyelet curtains, a brown refrigerator. Did she keep the stolen frog in there, with her Dannon yogurt and sliced cheese? Or did she have a freezer in the garage? In her basement?

We could make ourselves useful, we called through the thin wooden door. Steal more grenouilles. The boys who lived in our neighborhood knew all about catching small prey.

A woman's face appeared in the window, white and wrinkled as an old map.

"*Quittez*," she said and pounded her hands against the glass window. Leave.

We jumped, fell over each other's feet and legs. "Be careful of Marie," we yelped.

"Où est Madame Camille?" we begged.

"Elle est en Austin."

"Texas?" we shouted. Texas was seven hundred miles from here. Had she walked? Taken a Greyhound? Was she coming back?

"Where next?" we asked. Our mothers monitored our browser history at home. We heard the pings when we sent each other texts, knew we were always being watched. We took the bus to the public library, which was open until eight o'clock.

Frogs, cults

Grenouilles

French witchcraft

Frogs, witchcraft

We took turns typing and taking notes.

"Frogs cannot endure a toxic environment; they force us to purge negativity from our lives. Inner alchemy."

Then a site under "frogs, healing." Juicy photographs of psychedelic toads of the Sonoran Desert appeared. "Multicellular glands found in the neck of B. alvarius produce phlegmy venom that contains large amounts of the hallucinogen 5-MeO-DMT. An indole-based alkaloid produces an intense healing experience of some duration with no hangover or harmful effect." We typed "Sonoran Frogs/DMT" into YouTube. A video came first, a group of young people sitting in someone's dimly lit living room. One million views. Hanging spider plants and a burgundy area rug encompassed the circle. A woman knelt in front of a small shrine of a glass frog. A man chanted in Spanish? Portuguese? while a music track of rainforest sounds played over the audio. The man lit a stick and made three circular burns on the skin of the woman's neck. She winced but did not scream. He dabbed the charred skin with a tongue depressor covered in sticky clear syrup at the end.

"You'll enter new realms," he told the woman with the burns. "You'll be transformed. You'll never be the same."

The video cut to the same woman crying on a section of the rug. She held her knees up against her chest. She yelled something over and over.

There was another video in the same thread. The same woman with the burn marks was now sitting up, outside, wearing a blue shirt. "I feel better than I have since my brother was killed in a car accident."

"Maybe she was saying 'Danny,'" one of us said. "Maybe her brother's name was Danny."

"Shush," we said. "We want to hear."

"All the insomnia, the nightmares, my ADHD—it's gone," the woman said. "It's been two weeks but I know it's gone for good." The sun shone on her hair. She even looked lighter to us, like a different woman altogether. Her neck as alabaster as a swan's with just a kiss of pink where the burns had been.

We found more videos. More articles. People whose tumors had shrunk, cancers sent into remission, MS released from their bodies, all from inhaling or burning and inhaling the frog venom into their bodies.

We traced the name we'd seen on the biology lab frog dissection boxes. They'd been ordered from a medical device company in Michigan that offered single bullfrog and double bullfrog pails. No Sonoran amphibians. The science room supply area now had a heavy metal padlock on the door after school. In class, Mr. Haney walked between the black high-topped tables. Our frogs lay on their backs, throats exposed, on silver trays.

"Your specimens each have a bar code assigned to them," Mr. Haney said. "We made lateral and horizontal incisions. One of us walked past Mr. Haney's desk and knocked over a tray of scalpels. The rest of us quickly stabbed at where a gland should be, according to our anatomy books. We squeezed juice from our frog's skin into a thermos and kept it in Marie's downstairs refrigerator that her mother only used at Christmas. All week, our hands, our hair, our t-shirts stank of formaldehyde."

That week, when Madame Camille left, walking home from school down the long service road peppered with gas stations and nail salons, we remembered the one story our grandmothers used to tell us as they baked spritz cookies and pecan tassies. A story about an archipelago of islands, like the Galapagos, but more ancient. The women ruled without need for men. They powered great machines with their syncopated menstrual cycles. They grew great crystal palaces with their minds. They pulled power from the moon and sent the tides out and brought them in twice each day. The land was neon green and lush. The land animals glowed like jellyfish.

But all that power wasn't good for the women. They feasted on it, grew fat with light. The energy was out of balance. The sun was jealous and started to inch away from the earth. The male children's muscles atrophied, the water cooled, and the ground grew colder and colder until they all perished. The trees and people alike were like popsicles on sticks, stuck frozen until the highest tips of the land dissolved into the sea.

Jaqueline found a 1-888 number that took prayer requests. You entered the miracle you wanted into an app, and a team of prayers of some non-specified faith at a headquarters prayed on it for thirty days around the clock.

We pray our friend Marie can walk without a limp.

We pray she is spared from surgery.

LES GRENOUILLES

Marie closed her eyes and smiled while we typed. Every day she looked more translucent. Like she was becoming diaphanous, a little less here.

Marie's mother took her to the hospital for her pre-op consultation. The surgeon had rheumy eyes and a wet mouth. He lay her on the CAT scan table and slid an IV into her arm.

"I'm not any better," she said when she got home. "They're operating in a week."

We sent more messages to the Global Prayer Ministry, typing the messages between classes as fast as a hummingbird.

"I got this from Oneness.com." One of us handed around a xeroxed page of tiny print.

By the power of Mary, I draw a hedge of protection around thee

By the power of the Universe, I compel every cell to heal

Hundreds of these affirmations, declarations of health ran together under our eyes.

"They work if you say the mantras four hundred times a day each."

"It's crap," Jaqueline said. "If she gets the surgery, she could die, be paralyzed. Prayer can't stop that. We have to do the frogs this weekend."

Our mothers frowned upon sleepovers. "You'll sneak candy and rot your teeth. You'll sneak HBO."

"It's a group project for religion class," we cajoled. "We're drawing the stigmata on our palms. Making costumes. Writing prayers. Going the extra mile as you tell us to. We can use Marie's mom's sewing machine."

Marie's basement had faux wood paneling and a cement floor. One of us drew a circle in chalk. A five-pointed star in the middle.

"This isn't Wicca," we said.

Marie sat in her saint-blue sweatshirt, palms up on her knees.

"You'll be fine, Marie," we told her. "La déesse grenouilles vous guérira. The Goddess will heal you."

43

We were not *stupide*, we assured ourselves as we lit a hurricane candle one of us had swiped from the back porch near the grill. The bio lab frogs would not be as potent as the Sonoran toads. "But they must have some magic for Madame Camille to steal one, to risk getting fired."

"Besides," we reminded each other, "Everything we read says psychedelics are more about the intention than the drug itself. Some people think drugs are all placebo anyway—the *suggestion* produces the cure."

"*Un remede!*" we chanted.

The candle flame coughed and hit the side of the glass. "It's her," we cried. "Madame Camille is speaking to us!" We moved quickly then, assembling booklets of matches and the bundles of rosemary we'd pulled from our mother's gardens.

Marie had said nothing since we lit the candle. She looked smaller again today as if the doctors were shrinking her with a laser each time she visited the hospital.

"Here." From her sleeves she pulled two syringes. "Swiped them when the nurse wasn't looking."

"Unused?" we asked.

"Seal packed in shrink-wrap, sitting right in an unlocked drawer," Marie said.

"I thought inhaling the smoke was better," we said. "So it gets into her lungs."

"Injecting will put it right into her bloodstream."

No time to argue; we needed to go now. We decided we'd burn the frog venom into our skin the way we'd seen on YouTube. We couldn't be too far behind Marie. Any day any one of us could start to limp, or our leg bones could stop growing, and a doctor would open us up like one of our frogs.

Yellow haze. Frogs' medicine is yellow. That's how we'd describe it later, the few times any of us spoke of it, whispered across the pillows in a dark room with a new husband.

The scorch stick stung, a pink strike of pain, a sharp fuchsia bolt.

A throb—one, two, three. One by one we pressed the stick onto the soft flesh of our arms or thighs. We held our breaths as each of us took the gift. We welcomed the medicine of Les Grenouilles to penetrate our cell membranes, dissolve into our blood. Another throb. All but Marie, who lay on the concrete, her hair billowing like a mermaid. A stinging, searing feeling on the skin. We surrounded Marie, pulled back the white plastic arm of the syringe. Yellow-green liquid filled the numbered cylinder. It took us seven tries to tap the vein but finally, into Marie it went. And we went with her.

Levitating. We were levitating like the girl saints in Marie's book of saints. Inches off the ground, but still. So free of the pull of Earth's gravity. Marie, like pictures of the Ascension, floated higher than us all, all surrounded in gold and blue. We imagined her bones lengthening, filling with calcium and vitamin D. Like broken bones that heal stronger than before they broke. Her blood levels were normal, her brain a perfect spongy genius machine. We were bird-women, screeching, unconstrained, tapping the power of our dinosaur ancestors.

The roof opened up off the basement, off Marie's whole house. Sun poured in, drenching us in light.

Up there, it's a sun-drenched day with a perfect breeze. A yellow filter on Earth, around your heart. In it we entered the hovering place, between being and not being, connection and total detachment, orgasmic, unconditional, unlimited love. We floated down, slithering across the basement floor like snakes, scales for bellies, like dragons. That's how Marie's mother found us. A six-headed hydra linked legs-to-legs.

For the weeks after, we were here and not here. A fugue state, the doctors called it. We couldn't have hallucinated, counselors told us later. We'd burned formaldehyde into ourselves, dead amphibian cells. Nothing psychotropic. We'd imagined the vision, the yellow floating.

We didn't hear their voices for days. We forgot our names, who was president, the year. Then, slowly, some version of us came back. But not Marie. She stayed there, rising into that golden cloud, ascending higher and higher away from her body, out of the earth's atmosphere, up higher and higher away from the surgeon's knife, the brain needles, the Triptodur; until she joined a star nursery—spraying her light down over us like glitter.

TERROIR

On Monday, Claire was asked to write a story about anal bleaching. The request came via email while Claire was still on the train to work from her editor, who always arrived in the office at least an hour before everyone else. Claire closed the book she had been reading about the history of food on the Italian islands of Procida and Ischia, looked quickly up, confirmed no one was looking at her screen, and opened a new browser on her phone.

Some fast internet digging revealed:

- Anal bleaching first gained traction in the early 2000s after adult film actress Bunny Hanson had her anus bleached on an unscripted reality TV series.
- Cultural critics credited the porn industry for the outbreak of anal self-consciousness, but some say it was supermodels from South America and celebrity influencers who yanked the treatment into the mainstream. Kourtney Kardashian revealed she'd tried anal bleaching during a 2010 episode of Kourtney and Kim Take Miami, which prompted a flurry of online queries for DIY anal bleaching kits and creams.
- Last year, anal bleaching became a multi-million-dollar industry and spas in LA and Abu Dhabi began offering AB bachelorette and girl weekend party packages for groups of six or more.
- From Beauty Buzz: the how of the process: 1—lactic acid peel, which exfoliates the skin; 2—brightening peel, which lightens skin pigments; and 3—butt mask to wash off at home.
- The most common ingredient in the American treatment is hydroquinone, which is banned in Japan, England, and France for being carcinogenic and dangerous to the skin. Instead,

bleachers are advised to use the safer alpha arbutin or kojic acid.
- Warning: if done by an untrained professional, anal bleaching can cause herpes, scarring, and infection.

Claire had dreams of starting her own online journal—*Terroir*—after hearing a lecture in which the speaker defined that as: "the complete natural environment of a wine, including factors such as soil, topography, and climate." Terroir was used to describe the ecosystem of wine, but Claire felt terroir applied to other things too—including people.

There was a man named Bruno Travasio from the Sorrentine Peninsula in Italy whose family had made a lemon-infused liquor for centuries. He'd lost both his parents by the age of ten and was sent to live with an older cousin in London. Out of his displacement, he dedicated thirty years of his life to tracing the roots of his family's limoncello recipe and the origins of every limoncello recipe he could find. The point of the story wasn't the sweet, acidic drink. Claire would write about the man and the quest—the journey, the secrets, and the challenges he uncovered as the discovery of his terroir. Travasio kept his findings in a series of cheap spiral-bound notebooks that no one ever read, aside from his children. Claire heard of the notebooks from a friend whose family grew up one street away from Travasio's son. Claire had written to the family six months ago, and they'd sent her a scan of his entire collection.

She envisioned someone reading Travasio's story at 32,000 feet as they traveled from Pittsburg to San Francisco. She imagined people feeling closer to their roots, their ancestors, and to peace when they read her story. Her college career counselor at McGill, where she'd received her journalism degree, had told her the best path was to go to New York and to take any job she could find.

Claire peddled her portfolio, her modest clips, through Manhattan, to *Blue Planet*, TRAVEL, *Outward Bound*, and *Adventure*.

None of them were hiring. *Pose* was the only magazine that called her in for an interview. The woman who would become her editor blinked blue eyes over a venti coffee.

"You can write important pieces here," the editor said. Claire recalled an inane piece she'd researched for the interview, a piece written by this editor when she had been Claire's age: "Lose Face or Ass: Women Over Forty Must Choose." The editor had walked Claire from reception to her office full of brimming bookshelves and gold-rimmed glass furniture. She was probably around forty that day, five feet five of sinew, and lean as a preteen, arms veiny from yoga or weightlifting. She'd chosen ass.

"Give me a few months in health and beauty, and you can do a story on women's reproductive rights in Egypt."

Claire felt guilty for objectifying the editor's body and for not wanting to write about the global women's right to maintain possession of the very organ that gave them physical pleasure. She should want to write that story. Her passions were selfish, but they flared inside her, demanded obedience. Claire's mother was gone—a mean, fast ovarian cancer when Claire was a freshman in college. Claire's father worked as a manager at a canning facility. She saw him at Christmas and once each summer for a weekend. She was an only child. No lasting boyfriend so far. Her great joy now was going home to her apartment to read in Travasio's journals about the thirty-year search for the origins and tentacles of his family's limoncello recipe.

The editor ran Claire's butthole story with the title "Anal Excellence: 10 Ways to Achieve a Star Bum."

For the next issue, her editor assigned her to a feature story about men in their twenties with erectile dysfunction (ED). While Claire began her research, a rival magazine ran an article entitled, "Is Your Vulva Ugly?"

"Did you see this?" her editor asked and pointed to her desktop monitor, where the title gleamed in hot pink against a white background. Claire looked at a glossy picture of a girl with her head bent toward her chest and a fringe of hair covering her face. She appeared as if she were praying or bent in shame.

Claire stared at the article title and tried hard to place a vulva in her mind. She recalled Mrs. Mason's health class in the eighth grade—the pull-down screen with the string hanging from the silver loop at the bottom. The black line drawings of tubes and eggs, follicles, and a vaginal canal painted fleshy pink. Mrs. Mason had handed out small rough-edged mirrors the school ordered in bulk. She was a looming woman who worked in a bakery, kneading bread and pulling magma-hot trays of muffins in and out of ovens before school and the mirrors looked small in her large pillowy hands. "Take this home with you. Tonight, hold the mirror between your legs and get a good look."

Some of the girls threw their mirrors in the trash can behind the gym on their way to trigonometry. The mirrors broke against the steel frame and reflected shards of faces, legs, and backpacks up into the sky. Claire took out the mirror in her bedroom after dinner. She slid off her denim shorts and squared the mirror in her palm.

The floorboard squeaked outside her door. "Gracious!" Her mother was in and across the room in a flash.

"It's an assignment for health class," Claire told her mother. Her mother's eyes darted between Claire and the mirror, like a squirrel.

"There's nothing for a young lady to see there," her mother said. She sputtered something about progressive schools and pulled the mirror from Claire's hands, then turned her head away from Claire with a shudder. The way she did in the car once, on a family trip, when they passed a possum that had been killed in the road. Before her mother's fingers closed over Claire's eyes in that car, Claire had seen a rope of slick intestines, chunks of brain and bone, and fur matted with blood.

Claire could have defied her mother. She could've stood on the toilet and lifted a leg up against the wall mirror later that night. She could have asked a doctor to let her look during her annual physical. She could have waited until college and done the mirror exercise then—a million opportunities. But glimpsing her sex was now forever linked to something shameful that frightened her mother, something that left one flattened and bloody on a road. She'd never looked.

―――――――

Claire's editor tapped her pen on the screen of her computer.

"We should've done a vulva story."

"The Body Positive movement is going to kill us," the editor said, changing topics without waiting for Claire to respond. She paced back and forth in front of her glass desk while she talked. The beauty CEOs, the editor said, were afraid that women no longer feel terrible about their extra pounds. "What would happen to our industry," the editor continued, "if women didn't try to fix their rounded hips, their ass size, their asymmetrical noses, or add horse mane shininess to their hair? Everything's always changing."

In the pale light through her office window, the editor's skin looked slack and sallow. A vase of desiccated flowers and three greeting cards sent for her forty-first birthday sat on the desk. Claire had watched as the editor walked the halls at the magazine, poking her head, turtle-like, toward the chief's office, as if any moment she expected a guillotine to fall across her neck.

"Write something on the ugly cervix for the next issue," the editor said.

"I think the cervix is too high up inside to see," Claire said.

"Some other part then. What's that strip between the vagina and the anus?"

Claire scooped a word out of her brain. "The perineum."

"Right."

"What should I say about it?" Claire asked.

"Just look at some photos of a real one and write about how it should look the opposite. If it's bumpy, then smooth. Hairy, hairless—you know. I can't believe I have to explain this to you."

The article appeared in the May issue, in time for swimsuit panic. On the opposing page, ARCTIC cosmetics advertised a revitalizing perineum spray that tightened your nether region and made the whole stretch from your labia to your anus sparkle like glitter.

Claire's editor promoted the erectile dysfunction article to a multiple-page feature. Claire set up interviews with doctors, psychiatrists, and male-focused sex therapists. That same day, someone began a Facebook campaign demanding that toy manufacturers give Barbie a vagina.

"My ten-year-old asked Santa for labiaplasty!" a mother from Arkansas shrieked in a video. "She wants to look smooth, like Barbie."

Parents stabbed letters into the WebMD search box. "Labiaplasty is surgery to change the appearance of their vaginas," someone wrote in the comment box.

The next week, Eris Pharmaceutical launched Roo, the first erectile dysfunction drug specifically created for millennials. A doctor Claire interviewed suggested the epidemic stemmed not from toxins in food or repetitive sports concussions but from the amount of porn the young men consumed.

Claire flew to Happy Valley to interview a focus group of business majors at Penn State. On the plane, she read about a naturalist writer that wrote at the same time as Travisio. *Girl of the Sea* by Natalia Francone. Francone moved to Procido at eighteen and apprenticed with a fisherman from the Marian Grande. Like

Travisio, Francone became obsessed. She devoted twenty years to the octopus: its origins in cuisine, its place in the ocean's ecology, and sustainable ways to grill, sauté, and fry.

The Penn State business majors in the focus group confessed they'd had trouble "getting it up" on at least three occasions that year. For reasons, they cited that the girls weren't "hot" enough. One junior pulled at the strap of Claire's bag at the break.

"It's not the girl's attractiveness for me," he said. "I went home with this girl last month and saw her vibrator. It's that new one, 'Colossus,' you know it?" he asked.

Claire knew the device. Her magazine ran ads for a wealth of female-targeted sex toys: glossy pink pages with graphics of women with their hands down their pants, vibrating underwear, and women splayed backward with their backs arched and knees buckled with taglines like "Because you deserve it." Colossus ran on a glossy silver page with the single image of a giant fin. "Be ravished by an apex predator."

"Who can compete with that?" the young man said.

"Boys start watching porn as young as eight or nine now," the lead researcher told Claire from behind the two-way mirror. "They've never seen a normal-sized erection, a darker-toned anus, or an unshaven vulva." He shared his hypothesis with the focus group.

The young men agreed that they had been badly victimized.

Claire went home the next Friday with a man she met in a bar.

A beard hugged a kind face and a belly that stuck out over his jeans. He was not a man, Claire thought, who would be concerned with the attractiveness of her vulva. When they got to the man's bedroom, she popped off the lights—*nothing to see here*—wrapped her legs around his middle and groaned when she came. She did not think about the color of her anus once.

The man didn't call her. Claire wasn't too concerned. She hadn't said she was looking to see him again. She would have liked to, but she hadn't said anything.

In response to the nine-year-olds who wanted labiaplasties, a group of women from Philadelphia formed MAB—Mothers Against Barbie. The group partnered with Creata Toys to create an anatomically accurate doll with hair on her genitals. They named the doll Gloria in an homage to the great feminist.

The millennial ED article came out. Similar articles ran in *Elle, Marie Claire, InStyle,* and *Vogue*. Drug companies bought out premium ads during the commercial breaks of football games to promote their new solutions: UP, MillennialX, and Cheetah. Claire's editor congratulated her and sent her to San Francisco for a new story about an artificial intelligence doll that was popular among young billionaires. She rented an electric car and drove from SFO to Palo Alto to sit in on a focus group with the Young President's Club.

"The AI is called Perfect Girlfriend," the researcher from Synergy Labs told her. "They are life-sized and fully interactive. We're super inclusive here. The PGs have vaginas, breasts, anuses, and come in any ethnicity." She couldn't see his body inside the green lab coat, but the scientist was tall with a strong chin, fine gold hair on the back of his hands, and black-rimmed glasses that gave him a reassuring academic look.

Claire turned to the table where the young men were being introduced to their dolls. "That one is called Caroline," the researcher said. The doll looked like a friend of hers from college.

Caroline had brown hair, high-set breasts, and a mouth locked open in an O as if she'd been caught by surprise. "The mouths function like a real mouth when the AIs are charged. They'll perform any sex act."

"Do you think this kind of device will inhibit their ability to be intimate with actual women?" Claire asked the researcher. She'd devised the questions to ask from the research she'd read that sexual dysfunction in college-age men went up 400 percent in the past three years. "What I mean is, do you think these dolls will further contribute to the breakdown of human relationships and eventually to more young men with ED?"

The researcher shrugged. "They cost $50,000, and we already have preorders for three thousand Perfect Girlfriends."

Claire thought of the man she'd gone home with from the bar. The comforting hair on his belly made her feel she was somewhere natural and safe, like rough seaweed swept up from the ocean in Ischia. Would he have preferred the thermoplastic elastomer doll that would stay silent and suck anything for however long he liked?

The young presidents each hefted a Perfect Girlfriend doll into a row of private rooms nearby. The researcher brought "Caroline" into the viewing room and lay her on the table with the M&M's and pretzel twists and mini bottles of water the hospitality staff from Synergy had set out in a bouquet of glass bowls.

The researcher excused himself to the bathroom. Alone in the fluorescent light, for the briefest second, Claire had the insane notion of jumping up on the table and pressing her skin against Caroline's plastic body or lifting up Caroline's skirt to inspect her vulva. Instead, she drew her right index finger along the inside of Caroline's arm. The skin of the doll was nothing like the cold Barbie wax or stress ball pliancy Claire had imagined. The skin was satin, lush, and deep, as if someone had created real layers of epidermis, hypodermis, and subcutaneous. Twenty minutes later, a man in a striped Brooks Brothers shirt called them back to a conference room and asked the men what they liked about the dolls.

A twenty-five-year-old wearing a blue hoodie volunteered, "They're smoking hot. You don't have to go out anywhere to find them." Another man nodded and flexed and cracked his thumbs to demonstrate the repetitive stress injury he incurred from swiping on dating apps.

"It's exhausting," the young men agreed. An engineer came in to discuss pyrotechnics for the launch party. Over the chemical smell of the lab, Claire fantasized about dragging her fingers across a sea of lemongrass in Capri.

In the taxi, she thought of the photos she'd seen of the zucchini flowers Travasio described in his second journal—giant blossoms stuffed with salty anchovies and fluffy white ricotta. When she arrived at the airport, she found a bar restaurant that served spaghetti with Bolognese. She ate the pasta, ordered a fifteen-dollar-a-glass Barbera, and charged the meal to the magazine.

Claire slept with a man she met on the airplane. "Right time, right place," he said as he slid off her panties. She pictured the glassine eyes and puckered lips of the Caroline Perfect Girlfriend. She was aware of the freckles and hair that grew on skin, no matter how often one shaved. She pulled the sheet across her torso and clicked off the lights. She groaned as he lightly bit her neck. He came inside her. There were men who still preferred flesh, she told herself.

The nine-year-olds did not like their new dolls. They demanded their Barbies back and mobilized their own group online—Daughters Against Gloria (DAG). When MAB refused to return their dolls, the daughters set up surgical labs and gave their Glorias Brazilian bikini waxes and labiaplasties so that they looked more like Barbie.

"No more genital stories," Claire told her editor on her way to her desk the next morning.

An hour later, the editor's frosted head peered over the foam wall of Claire's cubicle. "Pack a bag for London."

She logged into the magazine research database from the JFK American Airlines lounge. Her new story was about Cryonics. The term came from the Greek Kyros and involved the freezing at -196°C and storage of a human corpse or severed head. In the hope of vitrification and, eventually, resurrection.

While a young boy in 32E drooled on the armrest next to her, Claire read that Cryonics procedures must begin within minutes of death and use cryoprotectants to prevent ice formation during cryopreservation. The first corpse (of Dr. James Bedford) was frozen in 1967 and as of 2014, thousands of hopeful immortals had made arrangements for cryopreservation.

Somewhere over Greenland, Claire found an article about the London company, Immortal You, which she would visit later that day.

"Yes, Cryonics costs upward of $200,000, but how much is that really to enter the era where science will bestow life beyond the grave?"

Her editor texted: "I know for a fact *Vogue* has this story too—find me an angle."

Greg Sommers from Immortal You handed Claire a clear plastic jumpsuit and gave her a tour of the freezing chamber. Greg was six feet seven inches tall and walked like a gazelle. As they moved into the factory, Claire's body, her handbag, her smartphone felt miniature, as if she were being swallowed by Greg's shadow and the refrigerated air of the facility. Pods of silver and copper lined the walls of a giant warehouse like metallic wine barrels. The writer from *Vogue* stood in the viewing bay, rubbing her arms in quick strokes. Frost crusted the edges of her press pass. "The thing is," the *Vogue* writer said to Claire as they waited for quotes from the president of the company, "do you really want to come back to a ninety-year-old body? If women really wanted to do this right, we'd take ourselves out at thirty and be resurrected with tight cunts and smooth foreheads."

Claire stopped having sex. None of the men she'd been with even texted her afterward. She found herself visiting the product closet at the magazine, her hand hovering over a tube of vulva gel. Her own body, with its coarse hair and gangly limbs and decreasing collagen production, had become a repulsive thing. At night, she dreamed about Caroline and the neutered Glorias and bodies suspended in immortality gel. Kim Kardashian's anus. She wrote whatever articles the editor assigned her: best sex positions to try on a yacht, anal beads master class, and how to find the new S spot that scientists said was up even higher than the G spot and could only be accessed while inverted.

Three months later, the researcher from Penn State emailed Claire. "I liked your article about ED. I'll be in New York next week. Drinks?"

She forced herself to go. To not go would be to let them all win—the editors and the *Vogue* writers, ARCTIC cosmetics, the DAGs.

The researcher ordered a small fillet, sautéed spinach, and a loaded potato. Claire found eating meat difficult now. The sinew, bone, and muscle repulsed her and made her esophagus swell. The man didn't mind. He asked to taste her baked squash and floury pasta. He said he liked the way her blue sweater matched her eyes.

She found herself telling the man about terroir, about Francone's Procida cuisine, about Bruno Travasio, the limoncello. "People think of limoncello as exclusively Italian, but he found similar families recipes in Croatia, Portugal, and one even in India," she said. Claire told him about how soil and climate and topography shape things—shape all life.

The man lay down his fork. He looked for a moment like he was many different ages all at once: a boy, a young man, a scientist.

"Did you uncover a culinary Pangea?"

Claire sipped her wine and looked at the man. She liked his hair, graying at the temples. Liked his questions. "Don't know," she said. "I haven't finished the piece yet."

The man looked at her in a way that made her feel strange, as if he were drinking her.

"I'm talking too much," she said.

"You're magnificent," he said.

They rode to his hotel in an Uber and he held her hand over the velour hump in the back seat. She felt the weight of his knuckles and ran her finger over a small callous on the pad of his left palm. The hotel was in Times Square. The lights from the marquees made rainbows across the small ceiling. Mirrored panels had been placed on the sliding closet doors opposite the floral bedspread. He saw her looking at the mirrors and blushed.

"This was the hotel the university approved," he apologized.

Her hand reached for the bedside light. She was unbleached, unwaxed, and unsprayed. She wanted the shadows to swallow them. He stopped her by the wrist and kissed her palm. Then each fingertip, one by one.

He peeled off her pants and unbuttoned her blouse. He kissed her clavicle, the inch of skin just under her ribs, her knees, and took off her socks with his teeth. He knelt over her and reached for his toiletries bag that sat on the nightstand. The lamp bounced yellow light around his stooped shoulders. She saw the gleam of light on his back in the mirror. She turned her face to the side, where all she could see were white fibers of cotton on the pillowcase. The foil condom wrapper crunched in his fingers. She lifted her head. In the mirror, she could see the pink soles of her feet.

"Almost there," he said.

She spread her legs apart.

And looked.

The researcher's long, muscled legs covered in larger curlicues of hair came down toward her. Beneath him, her reflection. A thicket of brown, tiny hair curled around pink flesh. A shining sea urchin. A paracentrotus lividus sparkling on a Procida beach. Dense and dark and beautiful, like a forest.

GIRLS

I

The boy sees me through the slit of his taxi window, a glowing vision bolted to the wall above the bar's entrance. His mother turns his face away.

"What is Ray's Girls! Girls! Girls!?" he asks, turning backward in the seat as they whip down Wabash.

The mother counts how many seconds his eyes feasted on me. The doctor who spoke to the school last week said it takes only three for a child's wires to be crossed to set the neurological pattern of sex addiction on the soft folds of his brain. Her fear leaves streaks in the air behind the taxi. *One second, two seconds—she was sure it wasn't longer.*

"Why are you upset, Mommy?"

The mother answers slowly, drawing out the syllables: objectification. For the rest of the day, she steams. Cooking cauliflower and filets of salmon for supper, she can't help thinking about any underage girls Ray might employ at his establishment and if they work there of their own free will or if—oh god—any of them have been picked up on the street in Green Bay. Branded with thorn tattoos and shot up with dope and bused into the city like the girls in that horrifying interview she listened to last week.

Reading to her son in bed that night, his body organic and milky sweet, she thinks of me again: a voluptuous tangle of creamy glass tubes, pulsing white thighs and blue hair, a pointy green bikini top that hides nothing. A lurid array, lit through with the colored lights even at 11:00 a.m., proving that the darkness never sleeps but always glows, even in the daylight. The woman cries in the shower that night and doesn't have sex with her husband for a week, in protest, in distress, in rage, in vigil—for the girls.

II

The boy saw me shabbier than I had ever been; my body is now an aging glowworm. When I first went up—oh my! The first man to walk by after I was drilled into the cement wall tripped over his loafers. Younger ones came in packs after school to look at me and point. The old old ones, and the barely men, and the middle-aged men in suits with rounding bellies, old men with white whiskers and hair in their ears walking from their offices, pretending to be on their way somewhere else. My presence was new and exciting to them all; my presence, neon charged, alive enough to make their pants twitch.

III

Women come alone, wearing belted coats and scarves around their faces and large dark glasses, holding secrets. They pretend to look at the menu of the German restaurant next door to Ray's. Bratwurst, schnitzel, *kazel spachze*. Sausages in the menu photos so long and juicy that the women get horny just looking at the pictures.

Make them want me like they want you, they whisper, faces pressed against the concrete wall beneath my thighs. They leave mascara prints on the wall, like stenciled love notes.

IV

Where are my neon sisters? the customers ask Ray. It's Girls!Girls!Girls! not Girl, after all.

They stop at the bar where Ray sits and drinks whiskey neat and the bartender stacks up American beer and watered-down martinis with small green olives on sticks. Ray says I'm enough woman for them all. I am his goddess. Back arched like a yogi, neck stretched long and inviting a bite or a kiss, shorts so short you blink and miss them, toenails painted '50s housewife red. The men knock their drinks on the bar in agreement and move into the guts of the place. I'm the first thing he bought for his enterprise. *All you have to do is get them in the door.*

He laughs at the fools on this same street who own fine dining restaurants and art galleries. Twenty-thousand dollar paintings and $200 dinners when next door they can have liquor and sex for almost nothing.

What about the girls who work at Ray's Girls!Girls!Girls!? a man in town for a trade show wonders. Are they really so special? Ahhhhh, he says as he wades through the tables toward the stage. Magnificent, ephemeral. Real girls with blood pumping through their arteries. Girls with pink hair, green hair, purple—not the millennial pink and lavender young women wear now. The Girls! hair glows fuchsia, electric blue, phosphorescent green, some effect of lighting? Their skin, every shade, soft as cashmere, smooth as lollipops. They are otherworldly but kind and accessible. The men can talk to these women before they peel off their bikini tops and gossamer thongs. The women give them good trading and business advice.

Who are these women? No one sees them come in. No one sees them go out. The men try, but not one will meet outside Ray's. The regulars joke that the back of Ray's Girls!Girls!Girls! is a portal to an alternate universe. One where the female species is superior to human women in every way.

V

Ray is older and more cracked than I am now. For his eightieth birthday his regulars order a cake with my picture on the top. The Girls! wear silver sequined hot pants and green cone bras. Ray cries—he is touched. His tears came out silver like the Girls' lipstick. The men say when you kiss one of Ray's Girls! your blood turns purple. Your saliva becomes gold glitter.

Ray looks far worse for his age, the men tell him. He's taken better care of me. His muse. There's change afoot, the men report. A woman may be mayor next.

VI

The woman becomes the mayor. She used to stomp in those marches the women held to protest entities like me. #EndPatriarchy. She does not like Ray's Girls!Girls!Girls! She remembers the great storms. The rubber soles of her boots the only thing between her and electrocution. She signs the old, yellowed decree that she promised she would sign if she achieved this office. Body-positive campaigns, respectful, conscious businesses. She's not anti-sex, she says from the tiny microphone of her smartphone where it amplifies to the fascia of phones around the city. Ray's evangelists make calls, call in favors. Free speech is free speech. Dancing is not illegal, Ray's crew shouts.

There's a lot more than dancing that goes on at Ray's Girls!Girls!Girls! but this woman will not be victorious. I have a right to exist. An army of women couldn't remove me.

VII

The woman from the taxi with her son signs the new mayor's petition on Facebook. She feels better and reaches for her husband. She pulls him to her and lets him enter.

After, her husband snoring into the pillow, she washes her face in the bathroom. I will see her son again. She can see her son a few years out, tall and broad and a little insecure still, walking sideways to my wall. Approaching cautiously, like a pilgrim.

VIII

One day, she takes that same street the taxi took the day she saw me. By accident, she tells herself, as if she is driving in a snowstorm, in a whiteout, and my street the only street she can traverse. I forgot, she thinks, about Ray's Girls!Girls!Girls! and that plump behind and lovely shoulders and all the angles pointing down, down, down to the crease in the short-short green shorts.

She thinks she hates me, the slippery gateway to porn and addiction and the corruption of all the men she loves. But if she hates me, it's for hoisting out all that she's worked so hard to tamp down, down, down, so deep beneath the neon street inside her bones where she tries to forget but can't forget, didn't forget, won't forget.

MARIONETTES

It had rained great gray sheets of rain since they arrived in Prague the day before, but now the sun was drying up the puddles on the cobblestone roads.

"My god," Kate said and pointed. "That's the third marionette shop we've seen since we left the hotel." She stopped and stared at the witches with hair sprouting from their warts and jesters wearing three-pointed silken hats with little bells on the ends—each of which was at least a foot high and far too frightening for a child's room. Kate could not imagine who would buy such a thing.

"Rain's done for today," Dan said, reading from his phone. "Think it's safe to continue on."

Kate's chest burned from the cold cuts of thinly sliced meat and cheese the hotel served for breakfast. Even though she was the one who'd chosen Prague, everything felt strange and disagreeable here.

"What do you want to see first?" Dan asked.

Kate's college roommate, Heather, had visited her boyfriend in Prague during their senior year and returned with pictures of a golden castle, turrets poking a blue sky.

"Prague castle," Kate said, but Dan wanted to see the astronomical clock in the Old Town Square.

"The clock is on the way to the castle," Dan said, thumbing through Google Maps on his phone. "We'll go there first."

They walked carefully, avoiding the deeper pools of water that rose up over the stones. Dan walked at least three steps ahead of Kate. She had to half-run to keep up and wondered why she'd never noticed this in New York.

When they reached a paved road, Dan read about the clock from his phone. "It's called the Orloj and was erected in 1410."

The Old Town Square was already full. About fifty people moved like a herd close around the base of the clock and looked upward as if they were waiting for something to fall out of the sky. The clock was beautiful, with golden circles and crescents marking the placement of celestial bodies along with blue sky and stars surrounded by halos. "Praha!" Dan sighed. "It's called The Golden City."

Still breathing heavily, Kate tucked her head down between the lapels of her coat. She hoped the people around them didn't speak English. *As if no one else there had ever picked up a guidebook and wouldn't know what Prague was called.*

The week before the trip, Dan had asked for her ring size. Kate had felt an excited stab of superiority when she called her mother to share both the engagement and about the European trip. Her mother, who told her going away to college was a mistake—that she would end up right back in Brainard anyway. Her mother, who she knew would be standing in the airless kitchen drinking instant coffee from the same sunflower mug she'd had since Kate was born. Her mother who'd had to practically beg Kate's father to marry her and didn't even have a passport. Kate waited for praise or even a whiff of jealousy as her mother took a big gulp of coffee and said, "It's such a big decision. What's the rush?"

Above them, the clock tower shuddered to life with a deep chime. Life-sized carvings of men rotated out above the crowd on a large disc.

"It's the parade of the apostles," Dan read.

The apostles looked down on the people, judging, and a woman with silver hair pointed at a statue of death that was now ringing a bell. "The figures carved into the side represent four evils and four virtues," Dan said. "The parade happens every hour."

Kate peered through the crowd where at least seventy had gathered now. Every day, every hour, people came here to experience the majestic gold wheels of the clock and the public condemnation of the apostles. The four evils bore down on them—vanity, greed, pleasure, and death. Kate wasn't sure how death was a sin since it happened to everyone.

"The Czech Republic is a very Catholic country," Dan said.

After the clock, they walked across the Charles Bridge, over the frothing water of the Vltava. Tall lanterns sprouted from the walkway like sepia-toned trees. On the opposite side, the road stretched in a long incline up toward the castle. "I can see it!" Kate exclaimed.

Dan pecked her cheek, and the skin on Kate's forearms reddened. She didn't want Dan to think she was one of those girls who spent her childhood cutting out photos of brides and reenacting fairy tales. She never even played with dolls after she discovered running and the sensation of shape-shifting into an antelope, first in the hills behind her house and then later through the mossy woods during a cross-country race. She'd seen a deer the day of her first three-miler. She'd won a blue ribbon and regionals and placed at state. Deer were a sign of luck, her mother said, and Kate got a full ride to Eastern Michigan State. She'd been full of luck until she tore her hamstring during her junior year. She missed the senior team trip to Portugal. The back of her left thigh was still tight in cold weather ten years later.

The castle road was lined with shops built of stone and old milky-glass windows through which Kate could see claw-footed silver candlesticks and Bohemian crystal. There were no deer, but the sheer fact she made it, through customs, out of the United States, to Prague must mean she was lucky. No one in Kate's family had ever traveled abroad, but Kate wanted to be like women who did. Her roommate, Heather, came back from her travels after lots of sex and drinking absinthe, wearing a dark plum lipstick called VAMP. Heather gave Kate one of her photos of Prague Castle at graduation. Kate first kept it tacked to her bulletin board, then behind a magnet on her refrigerator, and eventually displayed in a gold-leafed frame above the fake fireplace in her new apartment— the one she moved into when she met Dan. The gold castle was her new lucky charm. Somewhere in the shadow of Rudolph I's alchemists and magicians, Kate thought that perhaps this castle could bestow a benediction—a blessing.

"The castle was built in 880 AD," Dan said, "By *Prince Bořivoj of the house of Premyslides.*"

Kate pulled her arms in her coat and stared at the sleeve of Dan's sweater. It was navy blue and made of thick cabled wool that had started to go bare near the elbows. He wore the sweater constantly on weekends or holidays, paired with khaki pants and a certain kind of luxury loafer favored by every other young man who lived in Murray Hill and worked in finance. She liked the clothing she'd seen the local men wear here—wide-legged pants or cigarette-skinny jeans and long scarves wrapped three times around their necks. They looked interesting, artistic, not a copy of every person in New York.

"Hey, another one of your puppet shops." Dan pointed to a red doorway.

The marionettes at this shop were hung on silver hooks that covered an entire stone wall. Sunbeams danced off the dangling limbs of pantalooned clowns with painted faces, red wooden devils with arched eyebrows and long chins, and rosy-cheeked blond maidens dressed in lederhosen. A woman in a wide, linen dress with hair wrapped in a bun sat on a folding chair next to the door. Her hands lay slack in her lap, and her eyes flickered open every few seconds, revealing only wet, white eyeballs.

Dan ignored the woman and walked toward the shop. He pulled the leg of a wooden court jester wearing a red and purple hat with tiny bells on the ends.

"They're kind of fun," Dan said.

"They look like they would kill you in your sleep," Kate said.

Dan lifted a clown in white silk pantaloons from the center of the lattice and pulled the wooden handles to lift its arms and then kick its legs. The clown's mouth looked like a red hole. The more it moved, the more Kate thought she could see it animate with life.

The woman snorted and opened both eyes. Her irises had rolled down beneath her eyelids. She said something with lots of consonants. Czech was impossible to understand. "Come," she said in English.

Dan pushed up behind her. "Don't be rude," he said.

Kate balled her fingers into fists and followed the woman into the store. The air was stale as if water had turned wood to mold. A large thick table took up the bulk of the space. Wooden legs and arms, bald heads with holes screwed into the scalp for hair, and hats lay strewn across the surface. A male marionette with an Elizabethan ruffled collar and a deep blue satin hat hung closest to Kate's arm. Kate stared at the doll. His eyes were painted blue, and when she moved to the right and looked back, the doll's eyes appeared to follow her.

The shopkeeper jabbed Kate's elbow. She pointed to the blue-hatted marionette and then to Dan and laughed. It was an awful sound that crawled up Kate's spine. Kate could see the woman's gray tongue and many silver fillings, and Kate's breath stuck in her throat. She pitched forward and knocked the marionette from his hook.

"Darling," Dan said. He lifted Kate upright and guided her to the doorway.

The woman followed them into the sunlight as Kate bent so her hands rested on her knees. "I'll get some water," Dan said.

Kate grabbed his bicep and pointed up the hill. She could hear the shopkeeper's asthmatic breathing behind her as she pulled Dan through an opening in the stream of tourists heading toward the castle.

When they'd gone at least fifty feet, Kate looked back. The woman was standing in front of the shop, her marionette army behind her. When she saw Kate looking, she balled her hand into a fist, kissed the coil of her fingers, and then blew the kiss at Kate.

Kate grabbed a handful of Dan's sweater and moved like fish through a group of snowy-haired women wearing pastel raincoats and scarves tied at their necks.

She replayed the inside of the shop in her mind, and her vision pixelated. The doll's face and blue hat turned into kaleidoscopic images, then a shivering grayness, and finally oblivion. Her chest tightened, thinking of it. Even though she could breathe here on the street, she still felt off-balance. It took a minute to locate the strangeness. Her left big toe had gone completely numb.

"You're really afraid of puppets?" Dan asked. He took her hand and guided her to a more open space in the street.

"Marionettes," Kate replied, "And it was probably just jet lag." Had the hollowness in the toe started in the shop or after the woman blew the kiss?

Dan waited for her to answer his question about puppets, but she didn't want to explain about the marionettes. Her father read her a book when she was little. It was his mother's book, brought over from Germany when she was a girl . . . an old, oversized, illustrated copy of Pinocchio. The book had moldy pages and a sour smell, and Kate found all the pictures terrifying. The worst page depicted a red-eyed Stromboli, strapping a weeping Pinocchio to a marionette frame and forcing him to dance on a stage in front of a cheering crowd. In this version, Pinocchio is cursed by a black beetle for not being a good son to Geppetto. The curse is what allowed Stromboli to kidnap him and keep him from becoming a real boy.

"There is no such thing as curses," Kate's father said when she begged him not to read the book. Even now more than twenty years later, when something frightened her, like a knock on the apartment door when she wasn't expecting anyone, the image she saw were those bent wooden limbs, devil eyebrows, and Stromboli making his puppets dance like slaves while he laughed.

"It's not a phobia or anything," she said.

"Silly girl," Dan said.

Kate could see the iron gates of the castle clearly now. Velvet ropes blocked a queue of several dozen people from entering.

"Katie-boo," Dan said and tickled her hips. Her pinky toe was tingling now. *Was her foot falling asleep?* She shook her boot. Her pinky toe was fully numb.

Maybe she never noticed the nicknames because all the men she dated in New York were like Dan. They called women infantilizing names, drank banana daiquiris, and listened to Cold Play. Dan swung his arm and tried to catch her hand.

Yet, Dan had introduced her to sushi, ballet at The Lincoln Center, and indie films at The Angelika. Kate was attractive, yes, but inexperienced and midwestern bland. She worked at a physical therapy practice on the Upper West Side, where she lubricated the movements of geriatric hips and pretended to forget about getting her master's in sports medicine so she could work with young girls with track talent. There wasn't anything special about her, either. Thinking about it made her hands sweat.

Kate and Dan walked toward the line behind the velvet ropes. A woman in a beige suit held a clipboard. "The castle will be closed for an hour for lunch," she announced in English.

Kate kicked one of the cobblestones. Still no feeling back in either toe. So strange to feel nothingness in those toes.

"Should we wait?" Dan said. Of course, they would wait. The castle was the whole point. She could have asked for tickets to *Rigoletto* at the National Opera or the tasting menu at CottoCrudo. The castle would cost them less than $20. Just a little time was all she was asking for. Somewhere inside those walls, she would feel the luck and know her future with Dan.

A cluster of tourists moved like an amoeba to the shops on the left side of the street. Next to a postcard stand, a black awning stretched over a stone doorway. A man in a black cape faced the crowd and shouted, "Welcome to the one and only Don Giovanni Marionette Opera." He reached inside the cape with his free hand and held out a hook-nosed wooden figure in a matching cape. Violins whirred to life from a speaker affixed to the doorway behind him. The marionette flapped his cape across his neck and opened his mouth to "sing" in time with the music.

"Incredible!" Dan said.

"Next show, two o'clock," the man called.

"We'll miss the castle tour," Kate said, but Dan was no longer standing next to her. He had rushed to the side of the caped man. Kate watched him pull out his wallet and then jog back over to her on the street.

"You're mad," Kate said.

"What's that saying?" Dan asked, "Do something you're afraid of every day?" He handed her a rectangular paper ticket. Kate felt actual contempt for Dan and his sweater, his polished loafers, and his khaki pants with a slight pleat at the front. She had been so happy when he asked about the ring.

A tall man tapped Dan's shoulder. "Think you were behind me in the line, mate," he said. He looked a little older than they were, late thirties maybe. A long, willowy woman in a Burberry trench coat stood next to him. Enormous cat-eye sunglasses covered most of her face.

"British?" Dan asked. "I did a spring semester at the London School of Economics."

"We live in Islington," the man said. "North London. Name's Sean."

Dan shook Sean's hand.

"This is Annabel." Annabel bent forward and kissed Dan's cheeks one at a time.

Sean lifted his hand toward Kate.

"I'm Kate," she offered.

"Lovely to meet you," Sean responded.

"You're going to the show too, then?" Dan asked.

Sean turned his palms upward and replied, "If we don't see Don Giovanni performed entirely by marionettes, I will leave this life unfulfilled. But we're off to find a drink first."

Dan's sentences now lifted at the end as he spoke, as if he'd grown up traveling back and forth across the Atlantic. "We may need to join you," Dan said and pointed at Kate. "This one's afraid of puppets."

The marionette theater had a tiny bar in the lobby. The interior was covered in black velvet, and fake lanterns stuck out from the walls like arms. The four of them took the only high-top table with four stools. Sean bought them Pilsners from the caped man who now stood with a towel across his forearm behind the bar. As soon as she sat down, Kate's buttocks went as hard as her foot. Her breath quickened. *What illnesses started with numb extremities? Multiple Sclerosis? Parkinson's disease?* She thought of Heather's words about the dark fairy tale . . . about Rudolph's magicians. She thought of the shopkeeper's fist and the blown kiss. She tried to stand and wobbled. She had to hold the lip of the table with her right hand to keep from falling.

"Restroom," she whispered to Dan. She held the edge of the table to pull herself upright. Her left foot and calf were completely numb. It was as if her left leg had been fashioned out of driftwood, like in an old pirate story.

She walked through the dozen or so people in the cramped room, putting more weight on her right foot and dragging her left to meet it. The bathroom was a single stall, so Kate slid the lock shut and felt around with her good hand for her phone. No signal. The international plan she'd purchased was bunk. The lightheadedness from the shop was back. She'd heard of women her age who had strokes from taking birth control pills. By the time she returned to the table, she had to hop the final three steps.

Annabel had removed her sunglasses, revealing eyes the color of a lapis lazuli stone. Her skin was pristine and bright. She was so striking that Kate forgot the hollow woodenness in her lower limbs and simply stared. Sean kissed her arm then her fingers one by one. Sean probably didn't walk three steps ahead of Annabel.

Speakers mounted on the ceiling coughed on and began to play a staticky version of what Kate assumed was the overture of the opera. She didn't really know the story, but there had been something in the hotel visitor's guide about the play. "Devils drag Giovanni to hell, right?" she asked when Dan stopped talking to swallow his beer.

"He deserved it," Sean said.

"It premiered here in Prague at the National Theater in 1787," Dan answered, already on his phone.

Sean had seen the opera several times in London and recounted the plot as Kate grabbed for Dan's phone. Her right index finger was tingling now. She swallowed air while trying to appear calm. If this spread to her throat, she wouldn't be able to breathe. She hadn't learned the emergency number for the Czech Republic. How did one summon an ambulance?

The lanterns began to flick on and off. Sean dumped the remainder of his beer down the back of his throat. "Showtime."

"I can't," she said.

"Katie . . . Katie-Boo," Dan said. "We'll see the castle right after."

Kate wanted to run into the blunt light of the square. She didn't care about the castle now. She was convinced she could now feel the hollowness spreading across her pelvis. Her mouth felt strange, and her cheeks were hardening.

The caped man appeared at a narrow door. As he waved the black silk at them, cymbals crashed through the speakers.

Dan helped her up from the stool by her elbow. "I'll hold your hand the whole time," he said.

Inside the theater, Kate felt as if they'd entered a giant mouth. The seats were cream; the walls were covered in red velvet. Dan followed Sean and Annabel to seats in the fourth row. The stage was black and set with a painted façade of a staircase next to a building with a white balcony. The lights dimmed, and the violin music from the lobby rose and pitched. The air was cool and moist. Kate could no longer feel her feet or legs, and her torso was hollow as a flute. Even her scalp was going numb. She opened her mouth. She must get Dan to call a doctor. Her lips hardened like taffy as she wiggled her neck.

Don Giovanni's servant appeared on the stage, but she couldn't speak. Couldn't gesture. The hardening moved one by one down the knobs of her spine while the violins started again, fast as hummingbird wings.

Then Giovanni entered at the top of the staircase in pantaloons and a ruffled shirt and cape. Even though he was made of wooden sticks, he gave the embodiment of corpulence and wealth. Donna Anna slapped his chest and ran to find her fiancé. Donna Anna's father, the great Commendatore, approached. Giovanni drew a sword. Kate could hardly see the strings moving his arms. Even the violence was lovely, like a floating ballet. Such tricks of light! Giovanni lanced Donna Anna's father, and a ribbon of silk poured like blood from his abdomen.

Kate could no longer make a sound. She was receding into the hollowness. As the Commendatore's blood pooled on the stage, the thought of other things she couldn't do cascaded over her. Couldn't decide if she liked the Upper West Side or the West Village. Couldn't decide if she was moving back to her mother's sad house in Brainard, staying at the physical therapy practice in New York, or going back to school.

The slain Commendatore bent at the waist and fell to the ground. He was dying but still lifted his torso to sing his last duet with Giovanni. A delicious falling sensation cascaded through her head as the hardening moved inside her chest and across her ribs to a small cocoon around her heart. She couldn't tell Dan she didn't love him . . . that she didn't want to be married.

Kate couldn't turn her head, but she could see, hear, and breathe—at least for now. Donna Anna's dying father's voice was more beautiful now than any notes he'd sung before. He reached an arm toward the audience and to her in particular, Kate liked to think. The kiss from the woman at the shop . . . the hardening . . . it wasn't so bad really.

She could be strung up somewhere, on a little silver hook, and wait.

TARIFA

My mother told me the story only on the rare occasions when my father traveled for work. When she would take out a bottle of Drambuie. Only when it was raining.

"We were three girls," my mother starts, "on a road somewhere between Marbella and Tarifa, where our Spanish friend Seneca said we would camp for the week. We were eighteen that year. Away from our parents for the first time. This was before cell phones, the internet. When Americans were faceless, untracked tourists who bought Euro-passes and slept in hostels for five dollars a day. We wanted to take a bus, but Seneca said why should we pay when we could ride for free? Hitchhiking is done all the time here, she said. The boys we'd met up in Malaga had taken motorbikes and said they would meet us at the campground. Drivers always stop for girls, they'd said.

Esther was shorter and small-breasted and seemed the most put out about the hitchhiking. She still played role-playing games and staged faux martial arts battles with nerdy boys in our high school and carried around trading cards featuring girls with wild hair and lightning coming out of their hands or riding dragons. At each city we visited, she'd bought a glass figurine of a different female Saint: Aurelius and Natalia. Casilda of Toledo. Columbe of Spain. Her backpack looked like a doll emporium, and it was so heavy, sometimes I took a turn to give Esther a break. The figures were six inches tall and made of heavy milk glass. Casilda had broken somewhere on the train from Madrid to Marbella. The glass was jagged enough to cut a vein, but even though Esther had wrapped her in a swim team t-shirt, I'd sweat as we walked and feel Casilda's cut waist poking me through the canvas.

I wasn't carrying her pack the day we hitchhiked because Esther had been sulking since Seneca and I paired up with the boys on the motorcycles. We told her she was beautiful and lots of boys would like her. Maybe—we said—just put away the toys.

We'd walked for over an hour and hadn't seen a car. Even the airway up on the highway smelled of sand. The sky was purple-black as we wandered on an overpass, over some city I didn't bother to ask the name of. We'd left Seville a day ago. Moorish archways of perforated stone. Buildings that had stood for centuries, fragile as lace. Now, we walked along a cliff with no guardrails—fifty, maybe one hundred, feet above blinking lights of houses and farther out, the ocean.

When the car came around the curve, the headlights flashed twice. A blue sedan, an old one with wing-tipped fenders.

I can help you girls out, the driver said. Or maybe he said something else. My Spanish wasn't great, but I understood the knife. My brother had a similar one from the Marine Corps: a Ka-bar, squat leather handle, seven-inch black metal blade. A sour smell of old whisky came from inside the car, from behind his chapped lips.

"We'll just have to think of what you can do to thank me," the man said something like this and opened the driver's side door wide so that we could see the knife in the headlights and so it would be hard to get around him. Esther backed up so the heels of her shoes were right on the tip of the cliff. I looked up the road, beyond the white moon headlights. We could run, but he'd overtake us in the car. My knees locked. I felt woozy.

Our Spanish friend's shoulders hunched up for a minute. Then she began to drag the toe of her sandal in the dusty sand.

"I'm sure we can think of something," she said and licked her lower lip. The man's face melted. He drummed the hub of the knife handle against his thigh. I couldn't look at Esther, who I was pretty sure was still a virgin. Couldn't think about those fingers touching any of us or if Esther would jump if it came to it. I couldn't think what Seneca was doing, acting like we were going to go along obediently with this guy and his long body and sly face. Then all of a sudden, I thought maybe she was tired like I was tired. Tired of waiting for this to happen, tired of defending against it.

"Do you get it?" my mother would say and take a drink of Drambuie and the room would fill with the smell of honey and cloves.

Sitting in our small house in Madison, I'd think I didn't get it. But then, like a hypnotic suggestion, I'd feel tiredness seep through me. I'd think how I'd been tired since elementary school, junior high, since sleepovers, since watching the news, since attending the mandatory "How Not to Get Raped" training at freshman orientation week last year.

My mother would put her glass on the table and start talking again.

"Seneca pulled her shirt down off one shoulder. I straightened up my body and stuck my ass out a little bit to show how it filled up my jean shorts. I thought maybe it wasn't as bad if you invited it, leaned in, the way I'd heard a woman in a documentary say she'd done—when she'd been raped. How she locked her face on the rapist's eyes, forced herself to see him as a little boy who just wanted love."

When my mother told this part of the story, I always wondered how that woman from the documentary was doing now, if she'd managed to hold on to the compassion, the transcendence, or if she was totally fucked up? I'd think she was probably totally fucked up and how I was too, how we all were.

"He went for Seneca first," my mother would say. "Men always did."

I always got so tense at this part. Thinking about their friend Seneca and her long wavy brown hair, her long piano-playing fingers that I'd seen in my mother's photo albums. "He never saw Esther coming."

That's how I imagine they found him. His car door still open. Casilda of Toledo jutting from his neck, his shirt stained dark red, the keys in the ignition, idling in the night.

NIGHT SKY

It was just like Joyce to get abducted.

Not Joyce when Ned met her, but recent Joyce—the Joyce he had taken to calling Joyce Two. It was just like Joyce Two to disappear on a Wednesday in the middle of the night, resulting in Ned being wrenched from sleep by a shrill ring of his phone. He'd hurled himself into the car and sped the ninety minutes from Chicago to the Neptune Camping Park. His armpits damped with sweat, as he raced to what was now the pilgrimage site for every ET "believer" just because two years ago, a few drunk kids produced some grainy photoshopped images of lights in the sky above Neptune Lake.

Ned stood at the threshold of Joyce's small cabin—a one-story, one-room matchbox—and seethed. The door was ajar, the bed unmade, and the smell of something oily and metallic filled his nostrils. Joyce's father had been a naval officer and raised his children as if they were his new class of cadets. Joyce made her bed when he'd slept over, his bed when she slept with him, and even hotel beds with crisp military corners the moment she stepped out of them in the morning.

Joyce hadn't liked her upbringing any more than Ned enjoyed his evangelical mother's oppressive Christianity, but they were both still shaped by their roots. When they found each other, they vowed they would never be fanatical about anything, and if they had children (it had thrilled Ned how quickly the conversation turned to this topic), they'd raise them on reason and science and not indoctrinate them.

Taking a step farther into the cabin, Ned found Joyce's phone, flung down at the edge of her tangled sheets. At first, he thought the screen was shattered, but then he saw the glass was intact but bore an image frozen in the shape of an icicle. It refused to disperse,

83

even when he rebooted the thing. All her clothes were there, and her wallet was in her handbag on the cheap dresser she'd found in the alley behind Ned's apartment and brought up to the mobile home park in his car. The smell pressed against his forehead. He pinched his nose. She must have switched her brand of paint thinner or spilled propane on the grass in the back. He pocketed her phone, closed the door, and locked it with his spare key.

Looking out over the spindly trees, Ned's lungs tightened. He wished he'd never driven her here—never seen the beer bellies, the sad trailers with their faded red, white, and blue pinwheels stalled in perpetual sloth on the AstroTurf yards, the squabbling families who pitched igloo tents and faked smiles for Christmas cards, never beheld the Neptunites, the glass-eyed, not-quite-all-there, truth-is-out-there millennials who now made Neptune their summer home.

God, he thought as he paced the gravel path, he'd basically enabled Joyce's move. The way one would by buying beer for an alcoholic. He participated in it even though he was worried for Joyce and livid that she decided to leave the city—to leave him—just when they started looking at houses in the West Loop to move into together.

Ned was the kind of man who supported his woman's dreams, no matter what. He'd gone to First Friday shows at the galleries on Franklin Street with the L-tracks running under the pretentious tones of struggling artists and sipped juice-sweet wine from pre-school-sized plastic cups. He loaned Joyce money when someone stiffed her tips at the salon and never asked for it back. He even convinced his boss at the accounting firm to buy three of Joyce's paintings to hang in the lobby, despite not understanding abstract art. He drove her up to Neptune even though his body had revolted the minute he saw the place, like a struck dog. He arranged for her camping license online and carried in the boxes filled with greasy paint cans, frayed brushes in mason jars, and rolled-up canvas so heavy he pinched a nerve in his neck carrying them from the car into the cabin. He'd stunk of turpentine for days.

All of this he did willingly because he loved her, because their love was like living in one of those saccharine country songs he'd previously hated. He felt aglow after being with her—walked around for hours after touching her in a golden, gauzy haze.

Ned surveyed Neptune's toy-like structures, all dark and sleeping at 6:00 a.m. And though he doubted it, he had to be sure she wasn't shacked up somewhere in the park before he called the police. At the beginning of their courtship, Joyce would've hated Neptune with its pet psychics, the conspiracy theorists with guns stashed under their pillows, the crusted satellite dishes on the tops of the trailers piping Fox News into the brains of the residents. She'd never even had her fortune told and believed UFOs were bullshit. She was a six-foot-tall vision of copper hair and paint-spattered leggings that hugged her calves perfectly, a woman who read *Scientific American* for fun and worked at a salon, sweeping up hair, restocking shelves, and handing shiny magazines to women whose handbags cost more than she made in a month—all to keep herself in canvases and acrylics. She'd painted twenty-by-twenty landscapes, pastoral and cubist-inspired. She told him an artist needs to work their craft every day, and she never took a day off from painting. Ned admired her for this.

About a year ago, she'd said, "I'm going to a tarot card thing at Gina's." Ned had to think for a moment to place Gina. He could summon a kind of smudged image of a blonde stylist from the salon with three piercings in each ear and a tattoo of a rose entangled in thorns on her left forearm. Ned had never been attracted to that hard look, and he was surprised that he even remembered her name.

"It'll be a laugh," Joyce said.

The tarot reader told Joyce she had an Indigo personality and should be channeling a new form of art generated by her soul, not making derivative landscapes to hang in the lobbies of accounting firms.

"But you don't change your entire painting style just because some nutjob tells you to," Ned said when Joyce dragged all her paintings to storage the next day.

"Something's been off for a while," Joyce said.

Joyce saved the tarot card reader's number in her phone and began to consult the woman on a weekly basis. Ned never learned her name, but she recommended that Joyce see an energy healer to unblock her crown chakra. This led to a reiki session and a visit to an herbalist instead of a doctor when Joyce developed a hacking cough in February. Joyce always had a rational explanation of these things. Reiki simply applied quantum mechanics to clear blockages in the human body, and three thousand years of Chinese medicine can't be bullshit. Then there were lectures at something called The Astrological Society, and she had her own deck of cards with swirls of pastels on one side and messages like "listen to your inner guidance" on the other. Joyce pulled one from the stack each morning after making the bed.

"The cards are just energy," Joyce told Ned when he complained. "Gina and I are going to see a shaman next week," she announced. "She's going to do a past-life regression." Joyce took on extra hours at the salon to pay for the appointments.

Ned had seen women who would likely visit a shaman. He'd seen them in bookstores, on his college campus, on airplanes—women who wore full skirts with bells on the hem, gold eyeshadow shimmering in their lids, and dangled crystals between their breasts. But Joyce was sensible: a professed atheist and a realist. He found the whole New Age business perplexing, irritating but not dangerous. Joyce still came to his bed every night and reached for him after showering the paint thinner off her fingernails and hair. Until Joyce, the women Ned slept with preferred the missionary position in bed and wanted him to finish as quickly as possible. Joyce liked to go slow and smiled even when her eyes were closed, sometimes nodding as she kissed his ribs as if he were the much-anticipated dessert after a sensible meal. She was happy to incorporate blindfolds or a dildo here and there.

Without any discussion one night, she guided his index finger into her anus and moaned. Ned was shocked with pleasure and nearly came without her even touching him back. He felt intensely that night, something he'd always felt with Joyce . . . iridescence . . . tingles across his pelvis. Aftershocks, he joked with her. Sometimes this happened even without sex. He imagined he could actually see it sometimes, the shiny golden light. He decided it was the artist in her that made her magic.

The trailer next to Joyce's cabin was a single box, not too much bigger than a camper van. It had those same truncated curtains he'd seen in campers. Dainty lace, all wrong for the beefy residents inside. The call that Joyce had vanished came from Gina at 3:45 a.m.

"She's not answering her phone," Gina had said. She sounded winded or high. "I have to take my mom for a colonoscopy in the morning. I can't stay."

Ned checked his phone clock—6:05. He held his knuckles against the screen door of the trailer. Most of the people up here drank heavily (who wouldn't, living like this?), and he was sure to wake whoever slept inside. A wind chime clanged above one of the tiny windows. On the streaked glass pane of the farthest window from the door, Ned's eyes fixed on a decal sticker of one of Joyce's paintings, one from her "Night Sky" series. After the reiki sessions, Joyce's painting style changed from Cezanne-inspired cubist pastorals to something Picasso wouldn't have thrown up—apocalyptic night landscapes with skies heaving with fire and ash. Then a series that depicted a strange pastel underwater world where women self-procreated. After working her way through shamanism, witchcraft, conspiracy theories, New Age prayer, acupuncture, tinctures, quantum mechanics, remote healing, Rolfing, gong baths, and angel channeling, it only made sense she'd made her way to aliens.

There had been a handful of supposed cases in the past year. Profiles were carried only on the fringiest of podcasts with reports of "evidence" of five or six people who claimed to have been abducted. Ned argued with Joyce over it for so long one night that their asparagus had gone limp and slimy on their plates.

"They were runaways or serial killings," Ned said.

"But there's always that smell at the abduction site—high metallic, like a wind turbine. That's what the police and all the victims' families said," Joyce countered.

"When have you smelled a wind turbine?"

"Two of those people disappeared in Jolliet and another up north, right near where those kids took photos at Neptune Park," Joyce replied.

After the discussion, she'd taken the teenagers' photos from Neptune and filled a twenty-by-fifteen canvas with a hulking, bat-wing craft above trees with giant flashlight eyes and a mirage of golden light shimmering down onto the park. It was like something Vermeer would have painted if he'd been around long enough to read science fiction. The teenagers found Joyce online and promoted her work to their 1.2 million followers, and the park was soon glutted with seekers. Groups pitched tents, slapped posters of Joyce's paintings to the sides of their vehicles, and pasted Night Sky stickers on their rusting bumpers. Queen Neptune, they called her. And the queen answered by coming to live with her subjects.

"They took Queen N?" said the groggy man who came to the door. He had a thick black beard and wore a blue, brushed wool Union coat with the name Buck embroidered on the pocket.

"Masons might know something," Buck said.

As caretakers of Neptune, the Masons had the ability to sound a silent alarm, which summoned Neptune's residents like worms from an upturned rock. A woman wearing purple lipstick introduced herself to Ned by saying she was a "good friend" of Joyce and a practicing occultist. A reedy young man shrouded in a green hoodie and carrying a bulging leather bag said he met Joyce just last night.

"I host a podcast called 'Special Encounters,'" he said as he plugged a hand microphone into his phone and thrust the mic toward Ned's face. Mrs. Mason, grandmother of six, handed out coffee in paper cups from a tall silver canister.

"Makes sense they'd take Queen N," the occultist said. "You always want the alpha." A couple in matching gray X-Files t-shirts nodded. Ned's rage at Joyce rose to a whirlpool froth. Joyce had probably gone off on some vision quest prescribed by the shaman, and now he was stuck with this parade of insanity who would act—he could already tell—as an undertow to any progress he might make in finding her.

"I'm calling the police," Ned said.

"No police are gonna get her get back from where she's gone," said Buck.

As if on cue, they all lifted their faces toward a shelf of cumulus clouds that had settled above the lake across the spruce trees.

"The likelihood of extraterrestrial visitation to planet earth is infinitesimal," Ned said, exaggerating Carl Sagan. He immediately regretted indulging them with a response.

The X-Files couple exchanged looks with the Masons. Ned could feel their contempt (or was it pity?). He was the infidel among the believers. His back dampened with sweat. For a second, he imagined the Masons in a late-night meeting with Buck. *We could grab her around 3:00 a.m. Keep her under the trapdoor in our cabin. Leak the story onto the internet the next morning.* Neptune would become Woodstock by nightfall.

"To the cabin!" Buck cried.

Ned jolted ahead and dialed 911 as he ran. He barked the word Neptune and the street address between breaths. No way was he going to let Buck paw through Joyce's underwear drawer.

"Freon... metal. Just like in Jolliet," the occultist muttered. Buck dropped to the ground and sniffed the floor.

Anders held his phone toward the ceiling. "I'm not getting a signal."

"UFOs interrupt the tower currents," the female part of the X-Files couple said. "Always fries the electronics."

Ned felt Joyce's phone with its frozen icicle screen push against his left butt cheek.

"Joyce uses paint thinner," Ned said.

"Turpentine's made of careen, camphene, terpinolene." Buck

pried open the top of the turpentine jar and stuck it under Ned's nose. "That jar smell the same as in here to you?"

Ned's vision blurred. The smell was different, something grassier, high, and metal.

"No crop circles though," Ned said. He gestured to the ground outside the cabin window. He tried to remember the inane internet article Joyce read to him from her bath the week after she started painting "Night Sky." Real signs of alien abduction. Scorched grass. Temperature drop by sixty degrees just inside the landing zone. "How would they get a ship through those trees?" he said.

A woman Ned had not noticed before stood in the doorway. She was both pale and tan. Her dark hair hung in feathered waves around her face. She was tiny-boned and very tall. There was something avian about her. "The police will come to the Masons," she said. "I'll walk with you."

The woman touched Ned's elbow on the cabin porch, and he felt something dart from her arm to his, like a small electric shock.

"They all think she was beamed up onto a ship," Ned said.

"UFO crafts are a fantasy," she said. "Wish fulfillment produced by the human psyche." Ned had to look at her twice to make sure her lips had even moved. She spoke like a ventriloquist without a doll. At least she was on his side.

His shoulders dropped, and he grunted, "Exactly!"

They found a picnic bench with a clear view of the Masons' cabin and the driveway that led out to the main road away from the park.

"You've noticed Joyce is different," the woman said after a few minutes. "Special? You feel different when you're with her—tingles, euphoria, the sense that his body stretched beyond his limbs, particularly after sex."

Ned slid to create more distance between himself and this woman. He'd thought she might be an ally, but she was probably a friend of the occultist, as nuts as the rest of them.

"You're describing what love—I mean, what sex makes humans feel," Ned said.

NIGHT SKY

"It's different than that," the woman said. "You've known for some time."

Ned fixed an eye on the driveway and scanned for police cars. He was deeply worried about Joyce and sick at the thought that she was lost and dehydrated in the woods or being fed psychedelic drugs by some off-brand healer. He turned to the woman on the bench. Her eyes were brown, he noticed, like Joyce's. Her left eye was duller and didn't move exactly with the right eye. Perhaps it was a glass eye, placed there after an injury. He felt softer toward her. With those strange bones, her clamped lips, the eye, she'd likely been through some serious stuff.

"Billy Bob Thornton won't live with any furniture that was made before 1950," Ned recounted something he'd read online. "We're a weird species. But there's nothing extraterrestrial going on. Humans—regular humans—agoraphobic hoarders who dress up in mascot costumes and fuck each other in hotel penthouses. My boss's wife spent a month eating only kale. Kale! She had to go into the hospital and be fed through an IV to get her weight back up. There was a woman in England I read about...." Ned stopped and coughed. Joyce had shown him a post about the English woman. His breath was rapid now until he almost panted like a dog, but he wasn't finished. "She called herself a breathalist. She didn't eat food or drink water for weeks at a time. Said she was on earth to demonstrate that humans were meant to live like plants. All she needed was sun and air."

The woman had stayed apart from Ned when he moved, but she scooted closer now, looking ahead toward the Masons where Ned was distressed to still not see a squad car. Grass and blue sky stretched out to the park's perimeter.

"Interesting you use the word species," the woman said. Ned could not be sure, but he started to hear a hum in the air. Probably a generator had been switched on in one of the trailers. He moved another two inches to the left.

A black and white sedan materialized and turned into the

gravel in front of the Masons' cabin. They'd only sent one man, a young spaghetti-armed cop named Officer Daniels, with a pale, twenty-year-old face. Ned wanted a SEAL team—men with thick biceps and necks who would strap on scuba gear or drain the lake if needed.

Ned answered the questions for the missing person report and showed Officer Daniel some pictures of Joyce on his phone. Anders filmed the whole thing. Ned knew he'd need to surrender Joyce's phone. He was certain they had ways of tracing it through the cell phone company, and if he hid it, it would look suspicious. But he wasn't giving it to the officer yet—not in front of Anders, who would zoom in on the frozen icicle screen and get Neptune's residents in a lather about more UFO evidence.

The intake took less than ten minutes, and the whole time, the woman waited like a crow on the porch of the Masons' cabin. Buck and the others crawled up over the grass like stray dogs and helped themselves to more coffee. Officer Daniels set out across the lawn toward Joyce's cabin.

"I never told you my name," the tall woman said suddenly next to him. He hadn't seen her leave the Masons' porch. Her left eye was fully askew now, looking down and toward his shoe. Ned's mouth felt dry and his brain cloudy, as if someone had slipped something into his coffee. He didn't want to know the woman's name. For the briefest second, he imagined she might unhinge her jaw and emit her name in a language of high frequency sounds like a dolphin. He bunched the sides of his jeans in his fingers.

"It's Dahlia," she said.

Ned felt very hot. He wanted Dahlia to leave but felt unable to ask her to do so. Out in the grass between the Masons' cabin and Joyces', the humming sound grew as loud as a gale.

"Do you know Joyce's blood type?" Dahlia asked. Ned did in fact know. They'd gone online and made each other their emergency contacts last year.

"O," he replied.

"O negative," Dahlia said. "A very small percentage of the population has it. When doctors identified this type they called it unusual. Extra ordinary." She paused. "I'm O negative."

Ned didn't read medical journals, but he'd never heard anything like this and it was exactly what he hated about people here at Neptune. They made up facts to justify delusions. An interest in Egyptian art meant someone had been Cleopatra in a previous lifetime. A cardinal resting on a windowsill was their newly deceased grandmother coming to visit in the form of a bird. A smell in the air meant something otherworldly. But electronics froze, and people found certain books or art preferable to others . . . air smelled of things. None of it meant anything more than a bird, a preference, a smell.

The sky darkened, and for a moment, the blue melted into the color of a purple grape. "You said crafts were bullshit," Ned said. "Those kids didn't see any spaceship hovering above Neptune Lake."

"They are, and they didn't," Dahlia replied.

Anders lifted his camera toward the sky. "The smell is residue from ascension. People make up the crafts because it's what they want to see. There's no abduction. The only ones who travel are the ones who started out there."

Before Ned could compose a reply, the sound of wheels on gravel made him turn toward the road. A snaking line of cars, station wagons, minivans, old Ford pickup trucks, and cheap, used-up Hondas began to wind into the parking lot. Anders ran toward the group in the first car, his leather microphone bag banging against his leg.

Ned felt like he'd hiked three days on solid rock, uphill without sleep.

"Joyce was born in Springfield, Illinois," Ned said.

"Some part of you knew," she said.

"No part of me knows anything," Ned said.

Dahlia's shoulders pushed up the fabric of her shirt like clipped flesh-colored wings. The hum in the air died down, and Ned heard Buck growling at Anders.

"And you?" Ned said to Dalia. He looked not at her but fixed his eyes on the line of the tallest trees on the far side of the lake instead.

"We come when it is our purpose to come."

Within an hour, Neptune was active as a hive. The sun had already begun to drop toward the tops of the trees. Ned pulled his phone from his pocket to check the time, but the phone had lost power, the battery was dead. Someone pitched a tarp over four poles and erected a food table with a couple of grills. The air filled with the scent of meat on coals which covered up the odd, oily metal smell that Ned prayed he would never smell again. Groups of one, four, and ten moved from their vehicles and threw blankets over the grass as if preparing to watch fireworks. The sky glowed orange and purple at the edges. *Joyce should've painted this*, Ned thought—the purple light over the green trees, the blue lake, and the grass that would soon look black under the heavy stars.

"And your purpose?" Ned asked Dahlia. She was standing on the picnic table. He could not get used to the silent way she moved or her ventriloquist speech. Dahlia just smiled and looked down at him, this time with both eyes focused. Her pupils dilated and settled on his face.

Ned watched Officer Daniels jog across the lawn toward the Masons. The X-Files couple, the occultist, and all the others formed a blob in front of the news crew. Anders would ask for an interview. Officer Daniels would hand Ned a card and say to call if he heard from Joyce. The camera woman would shoot B-roll of Joyce's paintbrushes, dry and curled in their thick glass jars, and the sea of cars crawling toward Neptune Park with Night Sky decals on their beat-up bumpers. Anders' podcast would hit 100,000 views. Neptune would confirm itself as a certified alien site. Joyce's cabin would become a shrine.

Ned laughed until snot hung from his nose. The fatigue was gone. He wiped his face with his sleeve and listened to his laugh echo across Neptune Lake. The crowd grew from twenty to over two hundred. Someone hung speakers from one of the shorter oak trees near the grass. Country music . . . classic rock . . . songs about love—unrequited and lost. Ned climbed up on the table with Dahlia and slid his fingers between hers. They were soft and warm and long and cool, all at the same time.

POWELL'S PRIESTS

The spiritual lives of Powell's Priests were dubious. They drank, ate whole raw sides of cows, left the carcasses like dinosaur fossils on the lawn in front of the monastery. They slept with married women in the village, stole money, stung themselves with bees from the apiary, and on certain summer nights at the new moon, fucked sheep and dogs.

We forgave them this because of the honey. Sun brown, thick with waxy white comb. Glides down the throat like gold molasses and produces a kind of euphoria one could otherwise only achieve with something root-based and dark, pulled up from moss between trees, grown in a land we would never see.

Our only fear was that we would ever be without the nip, the golden swallow, the resulting spread of our bodies and minds, the temporary but sublime escape of our fears, our illnesses, our squabbles, our mediocrity, our settling, our aging faces, the shrink and swallow of the earth. So, we ignored the fetid smells, the flies, the vultures pecking in the yard, the squeal of animals on those hot summer nights. We forgave the graveyard bones, the round bellies of the women, the children that looked not like their fathers. We left the priests to their ecclesiastical court, to their consciences, to karma, to their reaping and sowing, and stocked the honey six rows deep in our garages, our molded basements, our pantry shelves, our kitchen cabinets. Like hoarders.

ONE MORE

If my boss, Ed, finds out I'm interviewing, he'll fire me. I usually don't lie. But I got an email about an interview with Good Media yesterday, so I invented a root canal, called the one friend I have in Manhattan to ask if I could stay overnight, and booked an economy seat on the Amtrak train from DC to Penn Station.

I find platform 3B. Smoke rises around the hulking trains. The smell of yeast and cinnamon from the soft pretzel stand drift down from the food court above. A woman in a red felt hat scolds her daughter. Everyone else stares down at their phone screens, a sea of thumbs pecking like hens. I'm not nervous at all, I tell myself. I've read that if you say something enough times your subconscious mind starts to believe it. I lift my left foot an inch off the ground and hold it there. An old superstition from third grade. Like not stepping on cracks or walking under ladders. I used to touch doorknobs twenty times each and check the stove in our kitchen in the middle of the night, but now I just do the leg thing. I stand here in front of the hissing tracks as if I'm not scared, as if two weeks before, the rapid train from Philadelphia to New York hadn't staggered off the tracks, killing twenty-four people.

The awful part was, I'd dreamed about a trainwreck the night before the accident. I saw the smoke and the scattered limbs along the track. This kind of thing happened once before when I was twelve. The night I felt the hot itch in the back of my throat, the night before the *Galileo* V craft burned up on re-entry. I thought the itch was allergies because Hurricane Amanda was slashing around the Virginia coast and the air got all humid and fevery. In the dream, I'd seen the Galileo pod circling the earth just the way we see on TV. I saw the window slide open and then hot orange flames, screaming men in the cockpit, and my brother was there too—with a broken leg. The next morning, I told my brother to be careful walking to school because I'd had a dream that he'd broken his left leg. He flipped his finger and ran ahead until I couldn't see him. When the principal brought us all into the gym to mourn for the astronauts, my brother tripped down the bleacher stairs. He ended up in a cast over his knee and, heavy on painkillers at the emergency room, he'd pointed at me and said, "You did this."

My father was concerned enough to take me to a therapist. I shook in the waiting room, afraid they'd call the police and they'd lock me in a mental institution like one of those books I'd read where girls started fires with their minds.

The therapist smiled and said my fears were poppycock. That was the actual word she used. "No child is powerful enough to cause a spaceship to explode," she'd said. "You didn't push your brother down the stairs." She told my parents I dreamed about fiery crashes and broken legs because of all the pressure they were putting on me to get A's and not have boyfriends and to play soccer even though I hated it so I could get a scholarship to Vassar. They stopped talking about soccer and college after that. I quit the team and they stopped talking to me about much of anything. They treated me the way most of the kids at school did as if I were a ghost. I kind of wanted to go back and see that therapist again but I didn't want to worry them.

Sometimes in the middle of the day, I think I see something in my peripheral vision. It's always on the left side, a waft of white, like smoke or the wing of a giant bird. I started sneaking my dad's portable TV into my bedroom and streaming sitcoms all night to make sure I didn't dream. I'd pinch my index finger and thumb together and sing happy birthday when I walked by a mirror or a glass storefront so I didn't see anything floating in the background.

Now, I'm worried it's started up again even though I'm taking the same precautions. I'm thinking about the therapist now since I had the train dream with the train collision and the doll bent limbs and decapitated bodies on the tracks. "Sensing something is going to happen is not the same as causing something to happen," she'd said. "What exactly could you have done to prevent any of it?"

Nausea moves up the back of my throat. I push play on Spotify, searching for nature sounds and Tibetan flutes teachers play in yoga classes so I don't accidentally think about the photos from CNN: smoke curling from one of the New Jersey tunnels, blackened bodies on stretchers, limbs strewn on the iron rungs.

I feel cold now, looking at the tracks that will take me into that same tunnel. After the crash, a woman from Union City, a man from Newark, and a five-year-old boy from Queens each independently reported seeing a figure—something luminous and cloudy pouring through the Amtrak tunnels, a white shadow. One of the online tabloids ran a blurred photo of iridescent mist, calling the apparition The White Lady of the Train. Why was it always a lady? All kinds of people died—men, kids. Why is it always a woman who is left behind at the lake, the cave, the train tracks, endlessly lamenting?

The article about the White Lady ran alongside the same twenty-pound baby, flying saucer photos and haunted campsites these papers had been running for years. Poppycock. And yet, for a second, the steel beams of the track in front of me slither like a snake. A hum runs through my middle as if the tracks are singing and my organs are replying. A mournful sound, like notes played on a pan flute.

I look over at the man next to me, then quickly down again. The tracks lie there, inanimate and silent as they should. The loudspeaker crackles. Boarding will begin in two minutes. Everything is still. It's just nerves about the crash, about the interview.

The silver doors of the train open, and I take a seat in the quiet car. Gray velour seat covers, men in navy suits and pink ties, women in shirts with chevron patterns and big bows at the neck. My phone beeps with a text from Ed. *Get some codeine or whatever they'll give you and get back here. The spider episode is due tomorrow.* My laptop is cold against my fingers.

Ed's post-production company, where I am a junior producer, On-Point Productions, edits reality TV shows. The kind of shows about people in Tennessee who train emotional support dogs and who also do psychedelics, kids with Tourette's who start internet businesses, and a housewife show where upward-climbing women in a certain city are launched into space. The Space Wives call each other whores and drink Skinny Tang and fight over who should be the face of the show's new environmentally unfriendly skin cream: Stratosphere.

In a film class in high school, my teacher wrote an email to my parents saying I had a knack for telling a story—knew how to use visual mediums in a way that made people feel something, to think differently about the subject. Reality TV had just exploded when I graduated college. For my interview at On-Point, I pitched a show that followed one random act of kindness to all its ripple effects. I'd start with the woman from New York who'd grown up in poverty and one year received a Christmas turkey from a stranger. That woman now feeds over thirty million people a year through her foundation. I'd find one of those people who decided not to kill themselves because someone smiled at them at the bus stop and showed all the positive acts they've done since that day. Reality shows are fake, yes, but I know how to be unobtrusive, get people to forget I'm there filming. I could do the show for under $20,000. Ed had grunted. He said I could make cheese-ball shows on my own time.

Over and over during my two years at On-Point, I tell myself I am gaining valuable experience post-producing network and cable shows. I am doing my ten thousand hours to mastery. I listen to Ed's jokes, endure his digs at the black leggings and flannel shirts I wear to work every day—you're a woman, Celia, you should goddamn dress like it. I force myself to attend the paintball excursions, the sports trivia events at the bar near the office, where Ed rests his hands on the waitress' asses. One night when network clients were in town from New York, I even forced myself to go with Ed and the rest of the team to a strip club in Dupont Circle.

"Why does he hate us?" I whispered to Jess, the only other woman who works at On-Point.

"He doesn't hate us," she said. "He hates himself."

"It's your attitude that's the problem," Ed wrote in my recent performance review. He highlighted "not a team player" in the notes section that would go to human resources. The remark stung. On-Point is one more place I don't fit in. Like Rachel Beaman's sleepovers, Monroe High School's intramural volleyball, DC Young Professionals. I think it's something about my face, the way my lips slope down when I'm just relaxed so that I look like I'm judging people. I'm five feet tall. I'm flat-chested and thin. I still look like a child. I make people nervous.

My laptop slaps against my chest. The train wails. We're above ground still, racing past dark brick government housing built up along the Anaconda River. I plug in the LACE drive that hosts the large footage files. For the past three weeks, I've spent my days intensifying blues and greens on a show about urban legends that came true—an escapee from a local mental institution who actually killed someone, a woman from Arkansas who woke up in a bathtub of ice missing a kidney, and a woman from Phoenix who used her iPhone to capture a hoard of tiny, hairy-legged spiders bursting out of a large cactus in her living room.

The "video" footage of the spiders had been badly shot on a green screen. I told Ed I am nearly certain the woman from the bathtub had a doctor friend gash her in the low back with a scalpel and forge the medical records. You could, without strain, clearly see the upper shaft of a penis on the X-ray they'd submitted to the show as "evidence."

Good Media is run by a female CEO: Cynthia Aimes. They only represent socially conscious and environmentally sustainable companies. On their website, Good Media lists only one value: Give A Damn. I've saved my interview time with Cynthia Aimes in hot pink highlighter on my phone. "I give a damn," I rehearse saying, wondering if I'll come off as a sycophant. I give two damns.

On my screen: the frame where the first spider erupts through the Phoenix woman's skin. Even though the stories are ludicrous, I developed insomnia after I began editing *Urban Legends—Revealed*. At night, tossing in bed, I'd be back suddenly in the cramp of my childhood home in Alexandria. I'm five, maybe six. I feel my brother's hand pulling me by the elbow into the musty bathroom with the purple iris wallpaper to play Bloody Mary.

"I will turn you around three times, and when I say three—you'll see the bloody, murdered queen." I'd heard of this game from girls at school. You saw your own shadowy form and pretended to be afraid. I squeeze my eyes shut. A tickle of excitement runs through my diaphragm.

"Three!" my brother shouts.

My eyes adjust to the silver surface of the mirror. It was the same mirror I'd looked in hundreds of times—every night when I brushed my teeth. A cheap, thin mirror, held to the wall with a set of plastic sconces purchased at the Home Depot. I expect to see the irises dancing up the wall against the cream paper, a slice of light from the hallway. My own face giggling and smiling back. I do see my face, my shoulders, my short neck. But I also see a figure glowing in that frame. No blood, no crimson dress. A white queen, hair matted and a skeletal face with eager candle eyes. My legs buckle. Before I hit my head against the side of the bathtub, a move that would get me six stitches sewn into my skull, I feel the woman floating toward me. Soft and patient.

My friend Blanca lives at 73rd and 3rd Street, across from a boys' private school. From her doorstep, the tops of lacrosse sticks poke at the sky behind an iron fence. Car horns and the hissing pistons of the garbage trucks hurt my ears. A toddler cries sharply in his stroller. I stand a foot from the door, trying not to get dirt on my dress. I buzz 3B.

A newspaper has fallen face up next to a stack of Amazon boxes. An image, obviously computer-generated, of an orb of white light

ONE MORE

floating down an alley between two buildings. The newspaper headlined a trio of male grad students who fell off their fire escape. Last week the Knicks had lost a game they were assured of winning. At least a dozen calls were placed to the New York papers about white vapor in the bathrooms in Madison Square Garden, on the college campus, in the alleys. "The NY White Specter," the headline reads. "Have You Seen Her?"

This is just a mind trick, I tell myself. I've seen behind the curtain. The media invents a villain, creates the mirage—starts connecting dots that do not exist and everyone starts to see it, too.

I remember what that therapist told me when I went to see her after the *Galileo* V and my brother's broken leg. "Everyone wants a sense of control. Proof that life isn't the careening, chaotic experience that it is. They want someone to blame, so they make up an enemy or they find someone to attack. The patriarchy is at work here too. Think about this: Why do all the hurricanes have female names? Meteorologists will tell you it's part of the nautical lineage, naming boats and avoiding confusion with other storms. Nah. It's Eve all over again. Give the enemy a name, preferably female. It's all contrived. Machines blow up; ships sink; meteors crash into planets; hurricanes lash coastlines." The therapist had talked so fast that I couldn't completely keep up with her. I felt as if I were in the middle of hurricane Janene, whirling like a basketball. "Celia." The therapist spun around and made sure I was looking at her face. "There's no nefarious presence—female or otherwise—behind any of it. Don't take it on." I'd had to look up nefarious.

I hold my finger on the buzzer and stick my tongue out at the newspaper. The therapist had been right. No one focused on the fact that the train engineer was sleep-deprived and working extra shifts due to the company's furlough threats. Or that the boys in the West Village drank Ayahuasca on the fire escape with no guide to watch them. Plus, I assured myself, I hadn't had a dream about any of those things.

Lacrosse sticks smack each other behind the fence of the school. A Mercedes horn bleats. I jump. I look through the glass again. Blanca's stairway is dark. I remember the day Blanca arrived in the doorway of my sophomore American history class when her family first came to the states from Colombia. She only stayed for six weeks before they moved her to one of the better private schools in Maryland. Blanca sent me emails from her new school and still messaged once or twice a year. I am always surprised to receive her notes. Surprised that the beautiful, regal girl who'd had servants and a columned estate in La Candelaria continued the correspondence. "You were the only girl who talked to me," Blanca had said when I asked about it once.

I buzz again. Blanca is there suddenly, on the stairs behind me. A yellow flash, like a sun, bouncing toward the door. She is wearing a white tank top and wide silk pants with sunflowers on them. "Drop your bag inside the door!" she sings and runs up the stairs. "We're going out."

I am breathing heavily, holding my bag in the doorway. "Maybe we should stay in. Interview tomorrow," I say lamely. One glass of wine gives me a pinching headache when I haven't been sleeping.

"You'll be fine. It's just a cocktail," Blanca says. "Anyway, we can't stay here. I told Dan his sister could get drunk with her friends from Spence."

I don't know Dan or Piper or Spence, but to say this would draw attention to my ignorance. The names make me dizzy.

"Cee-Cee," Blanca says. "I promise. We'll be in early and then you will dazzle Good Media in the morning."

The desire for this, to move here, to work with Cynthia Aimes, to have a job with integrity, squeezes my heart. I hope only to be just acceptable enough to be offered a trial position. Even one project.

"If you're going to move here, you should know people—these people who we'll see out tonight," Blanca says.

I smooth the front of my dress with my palms and follow Blanca onto the street. Perhaps here in New York, I will be interesting, not offensive. Perhaps here I will easily make friends, too.

ONE MORE

The black paint around the border of the bar door is chipped, giving the place a neglected feeling. Inside, the walls are black, the tables black, the floor too, as if someone poured tar over the place and walked away. Music with bass loud enough to make my shoes vibrate thumps through the floor. A single waiter walks from table to table, lighting votive candles with a green lighter.

A bustle of noise and energy erupts behind us in the doorway. A troupe of bodies floods the space around us. Blanca jumps from body to body, kissing them each two times on each cheek.

"This is Celia," Blanca calls over the music.

Someone presses a drink into my hand. "Where did you go to school? You're in TV—what shows?"

I put my drink on the bar for someone else to suck up through a straw. I try to keep track of Blanca's friends: Dartmouth, Princeton, Yale, Harvard, Amherst, Williams, Duke. Their lips curl when I say the words "Space Housewives" and community college. I could tell them that I was accepted at UVA but instead went to Northern Virginia Community so I could pay for it myself, debt-free. I don't want to feel ashamed of this, but I do.

The group orders another round: Negronis and rosé. The girls take their drinks to the far corner of the room, away from the throbbing speakers. "That's Aimee Kellerman!" Blanca is at my side, her lips almost on my earlobe. "Her dad is the CEO of Gucci."

The girl's clothes hang on them loose and fringy, like flapper dresses. Others wear silk pants like Blanca's, pajamas worn out at night. The sundress I'm wearing with its navy straps and wrinkled linen is so wrong.

"Onward!" a boy in a blue dress shirt calls out.

I check my phone for the time. "It's just one more drink," Blanca says. "Piper's meeting us at The Chauncy."

I'm wedged into the last seat in one of the black SUVs. The car lurches, speeds up, over and over until we are somewhere far downtown. The Chauncy hides behind a stone courtyard. Ivy climbs the gray walls. The ceilings are so low that most of the boys have to stoop as they order drinks at the bar. Alexander Hamilton used to get drunk here, someone says. Dan from Dartmouth hands me a glass of wine, and as soon as he turns to the boy next to him, I pour the drink down the sink in the bathroom.

Already I feel my composure for the interview slipping. I have to remember the quote from the previous president's speech about the way each citizen must choose to use their talents for good or evil. I search the bar for Blanca's yellow pants. Eyes closed and swaying, Blanca is slowly kissing a tall boy wearing a rugby shirt. Everyone is coupled or tripled in conversation. I look at my phone and try to compose answers to what I will bring to Good Media, my key strengths, the worthy and important stories I could pitch to their team. I'm as invisible or repellent here as I am in DC.

We leave the bar, walking many blocks past tiny restaurants, past lampposts flickering with yellow light, past bikes chained to a tree with handlebar baskets full of flowers, past dumpsters and shiny bags of trash, and past shops closed for the night behind corrugated sheets of aluminum. We walk across slanted streets and cobblestoned courtyards until my feet hurt and I cannot say what borough we are in. My stomach pinches and I realize I have not eaten anything since breakfast.

"Blanca?" I call out, having lost her in the clutch of bodies. She's near Dan and Piper at the front of the pack. Her long, dark hair swaying. I walk faster to catch up.

"You're so gullible," I hear Piper say to the Gucci girl. "There's no Woman in White roaming the streets of Manhattan."

"What about the linebacker in Pennsylvania—the one who was hit by a Volvo?"

"Didn't he rape his chemistry lab partner?"

"Accused of rape. The case didn't make it to the trial," someone says.

"She recorded the rape on her phone," someone else says. "There's no question he did it."

"In South America, we have La Llorona," Blanca says, dropping her voice into an alto whisper. "A weeping woman who drowned her children to be with the man she loved. When he rejected her, she killed herself, and now she captures lonely hitchhikers and eats their brains."

"So, the Woman in White is a zombie?" Piper asks.

The Gucci girl defends the New York ghost. "I hope the Woman in White did kill that linebacker. I call on the white lady to avenge the sins against women, to exact punishment for all the women who've been violated, neglected, abused."

"That will be one busy ghost," someone says. Laughter.

The talk of the white woman sets my body humming as it did at the train tracks. I grab onto a streetlight pole. I think of the mirror in the bathroom of my parents' house, the flashes in my left eye, the gleaming, waiting presence. The group moves forward like a parade.

We walk on and on, through a hotel full of gold-gilded picture frames and ferns and glistening chandeliers, then a bar in Soho with rowing oars mounted on the walls, and then a club the size of Blanca's apartment with glowing red strands of lights in the shape of chili peppers strung around whisky bottles. I twist away from the mirror so I can't see anything floating in the reflection.

"Blanca," I say finally when she unlaces herself from Piper's waist.

"Time to get Cinderella home," Blanca says.

Twice in Blanca's dark bedroom, I stub my toe. Blanca and Piper fall onto the small couch in the living room—a three-by-two-foot square off the kitchen. In the foamy air outside the room: the buzz of zippers unzipping, giggling, and then a thud as one or both of them roll onto the floor.

My sleep is thick and airless. Later, from somewhere far below, I hear a noise. My hand gropes for the phone. It can't be morning.

Not even a streak of light in the sky. The whirr of a motor. I crawl toward the window. It's probably a garbage truck on an early morning route or a van delivering food to the school across the street. I am afraid to look.

Through the dark window, something is there. Creamy yellow headlights of a car. Matte black and so long. The car pulls right up onto the sidewalk. The headlights flood the brick of Blanca's building. I pull back a few inches. The side of the car rises into a square carriage. A silver scroll adorns the matte paint. A hearse. A group of people packed inside.

Maybe this is the kind of prank rich kids play—joyriding in a hearse along the Upper East Side. A young woman I have never seen crawls out of the passenger side door. White light wafts from the inside of the car. She's wearing a polka-dot shirt.

"There's room for one more," she calls up to the window. I whirl and stub my toe again on the metal foot of the bed. There is no light in the room—the girl shouldn't be able to see me. The headlights halo her face. The polka dots bounce on her blouse. She waves at me. "Come on."

I lean backward. "No," I hear myself saying loudly, yelling. The girl shrugs. She crawls back into the car.

I pace the floor, waiting for Blanca or Piper to come into the room and find out why I yelled. To ask about the noise on the street. But the apartment is still.

"Classic anxiety dream," Piper says when he wakes up hours later and finds me sitting numbly at the small blonde table in the kitchen. "Fear projection. There's no way you saw a hearse on this street at three in the morning."

"Piper studied Freud at Yale," Blanca says.

Good Media is in Chelsea. I climb up from the subway and walk around and around 26th Street, trying to find the entrance to the building. "Forty-fifth floor," the guard in the lobby tells me when I run in, sweating.

At 2:00 p.m., I'm standing with a crowd at the elevator bank waiting to go down. Up this high in the building, the light is sharp. A few hours earlier a PA showed me into a room with Cynthia Aimes. I couldn't concentrate. My words were sluggish. I hadn't gone back to sleep after seeing the hearse. All I saw was my brother's face, his words after I saw the woman in the mirror: "If you see her, you're marked for death." My random acts of kindness pitch sounded cliché. Cynthia's mouth tightened when I said the quote about using my powers for good. "Right fit is important here," she said. I saw in the bathroom after that my eyes were red and cloudy. Cynthia probably thought I was high.

No one had to tell me I didn't get the job.

Women my age in blazers and skinny jeans swipe their phone screens, talk into their ear pods.

The keypad lights up white.

The elevator car is packed with bodies. Floral perfume circles me—something expensive, something one of the girls from last night probably wore.

"There's room for one more." I search for the source of the voice. She's there standing next to a man with a springy beard. The woman in the polka-dot shirt from the hearse.

"You'll fit," she says.

My calves begin to shake. "Next one," I say.

The girl shrugs. The doors close. I'm the only one in the waiting bay now.

The shrieking of steel against wire comes first. Then, dust, smoke, and burned metal. Then, screaming as the bodies fall forty-five floors.

"You're screaming," Cynthia Aimes' PA is saying to me as she pulls at my elbow and backs me away from the elevator shaft. I realize it's true. Who could hear anything above all that ripping steel? My throat burns. But I can't stop. I had backed away from the polka-dot woman the same way people backed away from me in the school hallways. The way my brother backed away from me in his leg cast. I let them all fall. I keep screaming so I don't have to picture the plummet. The teeth-chattering drop in the stomach. How long must the seconds feel once you know you will never see the crest of sunshine over a mountain, your husband's face, all the life you do not get to live? I scream over the peal of the ambulance sirens and the fire trucks until my mouth is only able to give out short barks, rasping and nasal, like a duck. The PA guides me to a chair and tells me to sit. "The police are on their way."

The tabloids report that the White Specter made the elevator crash. People search for connections between the Amtrak crash and someone who worked at the 26th Street building. *Weekly News* called it a death fall of revenge. The official report in the *Wall Street Journal* faults a rusted cable, perhaps gnawed through by a rodent in the elevator shaft. I walk fifty-five blocks from Chelsea to 73rd Street, numb, feeling nothing.

"How gruesome," Blanca says and pulls up a duvet to my belly button. "To witness something like that." Piper hands me a glass of water. I imagine that my brain is a fishbowl and Blanca and Piper can see inside. Once they know I knew the elevator was doomed and did nothing, they'll stop speaking to me like my parents did.

They leave the room though and I hear glasses being removed from a cupboard. Blanca asks Piper about a party he is hosting on Saturday. I sip the water as the glass bumps against my front tooth. The water tastes like chemicals, the sour tang of fluoride.

"We don't go to the Hamptons until Thursday," Blanca calls, as if she had just remembered I am still in her apartment. "You can stay an extra night," Blanca calls. "Before you go back to DC."

ONE MORE

I send my resignation letter to Ed by email, like a coward. "You have to give me this one more thing," Ed froths into the phone when I finally answer his calls. "Before you quit on me." I shouldn't have told anyone from the company how I'd been in the building when the elevator crashed. I'd told Jess though, the conversation like a confession, a weak attempt to dissipate the survivor's guilt that hangs in my chest now, like a flu. The White Woman had marked me for death, yet I had lived. "I let them all die," I'd told Jess. Jess told Ed.

"It's just like the woman in San Diego who almost boarded flight 357," Ed spits into the phone. "Or flight 1459 out of Tampa. The women—the men—whoeverthefuck was flying—they had a *premonition*. You almost got on that elevator, for Christ's sake. We need this for the show."

Ed is still talking when I drop the phone into a metal trash can on the street. I head toward Penn Station. It's On-Point's phone, Ed's phone, and I am not going back.

A thought is cusping as I walk past the bakeries, shoe stores, stationers, and pizzerias. I remember a television preacher I'd heard one night as the tv shoved noise into my subconscious. He'd had an intuition to take a different route to his church and on the way he got stuck at the site of a horrific accident. At least seven people had been killed. A semi-truck sent sideways across the road and one car smashed another like dominos. He'd leaped out to ask the police if anything could be done. Only the dead were left at the scene, he was told, awaiting the coroner.

The preacher was angry at God for putting him here, for guiding him to this place, if there was nothing he could do. God answered that he was there to be the light, to breathe pure white light into the EMT workers, into the families who'd survived, into the souls of those who'd just departed. The preacher had said we get it wrong some of the time. We misunderstand the role God is asking us to play, so we turn away in fear, and the miracle doesn't get to happen.

What if the Woman in White was like that? What if she had not caused any of the tragedies at all but had shown up to offer comfort the living, and to guide the souls who passed across worlds, like Anubis? Say there were others like me. Other girls, women, mothers, grandmothers that never fit, that dreamed things before they happened, that never got their dream jobs, their dream partners? What if there was no one white woman but maybe like Santa Claus, there were hundreds of thousands who didn't make planes crash or meteors hit the earth but were involved—or were being asked to be—like outposts of one white pulsing brain?

I stop at a pretzel stand. The air is heavy with flour and grime and urine from the enclaves around the subway entrance. Sirens, yells, barks, cries. This press of people and matter and waste. I could get a job anywhere, stop watching TV all night, actually stare into the mirror, wait for the next dream. I could call the Amtrak command center, NASA, follow people around with a soft blanket and make sure they made it through the day without falling. Or maybe I am being silly, desperate, egging myself toward delusion.

The F train rumbles under the sidewalk. The grates beneath my feet tremble and cough. I walk on, toward a striped awning of a store. The store is a thrift shop where the clothes hang by color—a wall of red, yellow, blue, and green. A bell tinkles as the door opens. The clothes smell like mothballs and Febreze. The fluorescent lights, like those that sent chalky rays down on my desk in elementary school, mute the colors. I brush past the rainbow of colors, the spectrum I've spent so many hours punching up and muting back on editing bay screens. I go all the way to the back wall, past the wire racks of blue jeans, the coal-black hoodies, the leather jackets, and the studded collars. I reach my fingers into dresses of snow, of cotton, and of linen, looking for one that smells fresh and real-looking for something white.

SALAD

That actress who won that Oscar last year launched a salad dressing line today. Not that actress. The other one. The redhead who married that guy from the Stanley Kubrick movie and then disappeared to Thailand and then it came out that she was bipolar. Okay, fine—is bipolar. It's kind of crappy when medical companies label people—like the condition is their identity and not just a disease they have. Well, she wasn't even bipolar.

It turned out she had fibromyalgia—has fibromyalgia—and once she found out she raised all that money for people with fibromyalgia. Yeah, she's the one who cut her hair live on TikTok with Beyonce playing in the background. No, I don't really know what fibromyalgia is. I think it's some kind of nerve disorder where you feel like your body is on fire. Wait, no, I think it's actually a kind of autoimmune condition—like Lyme disease. I can't stand that the internet is down so I can't google anything.

You do, too, know about Lyme disease. It's the one you get from bats—or owls—no wait, ticks. Deer ticks, I think, the large kind in the woods on the East Coast.

Well, I'm not saying you can't get Lyme disease in California. There's that other celebrity who got it in Quebec—the one who was in the circus movie with the actor from Namibia—so I'm sure you *can* get it anywhere. Just more people get it up in the Adirondacks and the Cape and in Maine and places like that.

Yeah? Yeah, so the salad dressing is going to be this Skinny Star line of creamy dressings: Green Goddess, Magic Ranch, Grecian Thousand Island. They're going to have all these superfood injections like L-lysine and HCL and chia seeds and two million probiotics per tablespoon. And they're supposed to taste so good, like real olive oil and mayonnaise, but they are made with this new technology where your body passes the fat molecules through to your large intestine—intact. Super futuristic. You just pass the fat out and don't gain a pound.

It is kind of like those Olestra Doritos back in the nineties. I know Olestra gave people diarrhea and hemorrhoids, but it also let me eat supersized bags of Cool Ranch chips without gaining weight, so I was okay running to the bathroom a few extra times a day.

The salad dressings she's doing—what? No, I still can't remember her last name and my Wi-Fi connection still says "unstable," but you totally know her. She was in three movies last year. Tall, dramatic face. Wore that crazy dress to the Oscars, where the slit went right up the front to her fuchsia thong. I know everybody semi-famous wants to get into lifestyle products so they can make uber money but the salad dressings really do sound cool. It was supposedly an accident, but her team tested them during the Invetid pandemic and one of those doctors from the show *Doctors* is coming out for the launch saying each dressing also creates these superbugs—no, not like eating crickets for the protein—these are some kind of white blood cell accelerators that could fight off even the most terrifying virus. Eating them gives you some kind of hyper-immunity.

Even if it's not true, it's good marketing, you know? Everyone will stock their bunkers and garages with cases of the stuff. No, the internet went down just as I was about to pre-order. They'll probably be sold out when I get back on. I don't watch QVC or any of that garbage, but this was on my Facebook feed three days in a row and the name caught me, you know? Skinny Star.

I'm going to try to get the multi-pack with all the flavors.

Yeah, I'm still here. I was just thinking, I wish I could launch some perfume or cereal or skin care cream. No one would buy it if I did, of course. It's just amazing how these stars go on one pregnancy or wife-swap show or do a small movie and they're Paul Newman with a salad dressing empire.

Yeah, Paul Newman did give all his money to those hard-of-hearing kids at those camps. He is such a good person. Or was. I

SALAD

think he died last year. Or maybe the camp was for kids with physical disabilities or kids with albinism—you know, the ones with pink skin that need the special glasses. Oh, it was just for regular kids? Am sure it was for underprivileged kids at least—otherwise, why couldn't their own parents pay for it? No, I never went to camp. Are you kidding? Arlette and Sam Jamison springing for acting camp or summer robotics—I don't think so.

The internet says it's reloading, but I don't know. The site says it may take over an hour. I don't have a TV anymore. And I like watching *Law & Order*: SVU on my laptop while I go to sleep. Is it sick? I don't know. Seeing Dick Wolf's name and hearing those synthesizer bongs, Mariska Hargitay almost always catches the bad guy. I'm like one of Pavlov's dogs with that show. Third bong, and I'm out, drooling on the pillowcase. Well, yeah, the meds make me sleepy. I still want to come off them.

For sure. Of course. I know you have to work. I'll order you the multipack of the dressings too—soon as the internet's back. It's like $100 for the full case. My disability payments won't cover that, but I have a bit extra since I've been inside for a few weeks. I can't go out too many places when the shaking gets bad. No, my doctors don't know what brings it on.

The smaller multipack of the dressings is like $50 or something. You can Venmo me.

It's amazing when you consider it, though. Caro, Caroline, Cynthia—it's something with a C. She's my same age. Before the internet went down, I went to her Instagram page. She grew up in New Jersey just like me and now she's going to be making seven figures a year on salad dressing. I know, Bethany from *Real Housewives* of NYC sold the Skinny Margaritas for $1.2 billion. So, C will probably make a billion. I couldn't go out and do any of that because of not being famous and the shaking and my foot. I think it makes people uncomfortable.

Yeah, it's still too swollen to wear shoes. I can wear those puffy snow boot things—that's about it these days. I get it, of course.

Optics are everything. I don't look the part. It's funny because I don't even notice the shaking so I never think it's that bad. And now so many people do business virtually, so I thought I could come back to the firm this year and work remotely. No one would see me, aside from in that little rectangular box on their screen, and you can't see a hand shaking or my puffed-up foot in an email, but they said it's just not a good fit—or maybe they said it wasn't a good time—something like that.

Totally. Put me on hold.

You're back? I was saying, you know, before my internet went down, I clicked on C's Instagram account as I told you; I can't believe I can't remember her name—I think it's my new medication. She went to the high school two towns over from mine! Ardsley High School Panthers. We played them in football every year. She and I were both in the drama club at our schools. We're close to the same height, according to her IMDb page. It's just so strange, you know? I even did a commercial once when I was fourteen. I didn't tell you? Just like C did when she was in eighth grade. I got picked out of over a thousand girls in New York City. It was for Shine Hard toothpaste and the casting director couldn't believe I had such straight, gleaming teeth without having braces or having them whitened. "Good genes!" she said like she was saying, "Great guns!" She called me Gene for the whole shoot after that. I got the lead in every school play too.

C's page said she played Dorothy, Eponine, Belle—all the leads in her plays as well. Well, right, sure—I got the leads in the plays until senior year. When the shakes started. That week before I took the SATs. Just came on like a fever. My parents dragged me into the shower at eight in the morning, running the water on ice-cold, trying to wake me up, but they couldn't. No one could. For the next four months, I'd be out like I was in a coma most of the day and then awake from eleven to five a.m., like they'd stuck me with a cattle prod.

It is crazy. I know. The world is crazy. My doctors said it was brought on by hormones—it's just the way late puberty hits some people's brains. They sent me to a chat room with kids who'd had psychotic breaks, schizophrenia, category I epilepsy, manic depression. This one kid was having grand mal seizures like ten times a day his freshman year of college. I guess I got off pretty lucky compared to that.

But at fourteen, she and I were two long, blond girls with good genes, picked from among thousands, shining on a stage.

No, internet's still not up. How is your chicken? I haven't done cumin-crusted thighs. I'm allergic to so much now. I do like that guy on The Food Network, though. I liked how he taught Pantry Meals every day on YouTube when we had the Invetid virus. Think, even if you didn't cook them, the videos made you feel less lonely. I'm sending you a screenshot of the dressings so you can see what they look like.

Before my internet went down, I found C's house on Google Earth. Of course, her current house now is in LA—probably the Hollywood Hills—*The Hills*. I looked up the house she lived in when she went to high school. According to an article I found in *Variety*, her parents still live in Ardsley. Their house is only two miles from mine! I've totally driven right past it. There's a big Target on Ashford Avenue. Her mom is on Facebook. Found her account right away. There was a picture of C in front of the house so I know it's the same one. She has all these posts about C's movies and, of course, today with the launch, the salad dressings. I was thinking about how my parents would get such a kick out of it if someone from my high school got in touch with them to say something nice about me. Most of her friends probably moved to the city or to LA, but I'm still here.

I thought that when the dressings arrived, I would make up a nice cobb or California kale and drive over there one day. Show her mother how much I appreciate her daughter's success. My mother would like that if someone did it for me. I mean, of course, no one would, since I'm not famous, but if I was. I understand it could be awkward since I haven't seen C's mother since high school. Well, I mean, I never saw her, exactly, but all the moms in this area are basically the same. Button-down shirts, jeans, Coach bags, J.Crew sweaters. They really live for their kids here. It's why my mom got so depressed, I think. National Merit Scholar on the way to the Ivy's to shut in. It's not really something she can talk about when she runs into someone at Grand Union.

C's mom's Facebook page showed her going to the Oscars with C last year. I like that, when a celebrity isn't dating someone and they take their parent. Like when Leonardo DiCaprio took his dad—or maybe Brad Pitt took his dad—or some really incredibly gorgeous guy took his dad one of those years. Her mom wore this black sequined dress by Vera Wang and she really looked nice. My mother doesn't go out anymore. She wears shorts from Target or the bathrobe I gave her ten years ago.

I was just thinking when you were eating dinner that I wouldn't have to really wait until the dressings arrive. I can throw together a salad and bring it to C's mom. Or some brownies. Or a cake. I'm really good at salads. I know how to make radish curls from watching one of those Cook like a Caterer videos on YouTube. I checked and I have enough gas to make it over there.

I'm here now. Right out front—9345 Elmdale Lane. Nine-thirty isn't that late. I'll just say congratulations and if they invite me in, I'll say how I sort of knew their daughter. I'm sure they'll be thankful to hear that another person is ordering two $100 cases of her salad dressing on the day they went on sale. I mean, what parent wouldn't want to hear that? Especially from a friend of their daughter.

UNENDING DAY

The clock at Macy's on State Street has been stuck at four o'clock for months. It's nearly five now and Dr. Levine stares at you, long and uncomfortable, if you're late. I double my pace and stare up at the oxidized copper curlicues that surround the clock's glowing face. I know it's been stuck for at least four months because I pass it every Tuesday and Thursday on the way to Dr. Levine's office after my work day at the Lewis College library. I went in and complained at Macy's once. Walked seven floors up to customer service near the gift wrap department and the bald-looking space that stocks a few leftover Christmas ornaments year-round.

"That clock is over one hundred years old," a man in a sweater vest told me. "The parts have to come from Germany. We don't have the right tools to fix it."

Four o'clock, the worst time of day. An hour that ushers in gloom. In Chicago, in March, the day is dark at the edges by four.

I walk into the lobby, art deco gold embellishments, lots of smoked glass. Like Vegas or a fever dream, a place so dense and contained it seems that no time passes here at all. My mother's face appears on my phone. A photo of her in a sunhat from five years ago when we went to the Chesapeake Bay to eat blue crabs. I don't pick it up. Dr. Levine warns us against talking to our parents.

Dr. Levine's office on the eighteenth floor is painted putty white. The carpet is gray, industrial. A decorator, analyzing the space, might think the inhabitant is colorblind, or a robot. Dr. Levine claims the atmosphere is intentional. Framed art or decorative lamps or pillows distract patients. The bare walls and high-backed black spaceship command center chairs, she says, are meant to act as a blank canvas for her patients' subconscious.

The group to which I have been assigned is for people who've experienced *extreme trauma*. And Dr. Levine thinks I'm hyperbolic. Dr. Levine insisted I sign a confidentiality waiver, which lets her report on my progress to my boss, Roxanne, each Monday. When I realized what I'd gotten into, I tried to switch to another therapist, but Dr. Levine told my boss that switching was an avoidance tactic, a "red flag." Roxanne showed me the email and made me commit in writing that I would stick with the group.

It is Thursday today and I sigh before taking my seat in the chair with the loose wheel, facing the window and the stuck clock. The rest of the group includes Daniel (raised in a Jehovah's Witness cult), also Tim (an anorexic/binge eater, a slack-skinned golem of a man during the half of the year when he drinks only Slim Quick protein shakes twice a day and then—according to what I've heard from Annie, who joined the group before me—balloons his way up a couple hundred pounds like a whale in the summer months). I both do and do not look forward to seeing this metamorphosis.

Annie is next. Dandelion hair and cartoon-big eyes. She told the group that when she was a baby, her father threw her against a wall. She giggles constantly and wears sweatshirts with handprints and sunflowers that she paints herself with puffy fabric paints. She always speaks in a singsong way like a nursery rhyme. She told me her voice was not impacted by the brain injury from the wall, but I am not convinced. When I hear the baby sound of her voice and watch the waxed look of her skin as her mouth moves, I dig my nails into the cheeks of my palms to keep from screaming.

In the next chair is a woman named Peabo. Peabo works in marketing for a record label and does cocaine with the studio guys, and a while back, when a famous musician came in and thought she was a prostitute, went along with it and had sex in the sound booth. For three hundred dollars. Now, she finds she can't enjoy sex unless she gets paid for it—even though she doesn't need the money.

Keesha is the final member. I don't know what her issue is. She never talks and Dr. Levine never makes her. She's had only one outburst in four months and that was the day she yelled at Peabo for thwarting progress for Black women. She said Peabo was reenacting slavery in her behavior with white men in positions of power. Peabo screamed back that *slaves didn't get paid* and threatened to throw Keesha and her chair out the window. Bunch of sickos, I think, every time I'm here.

We sit in this order, the same chairs, the same view, every session. Traumatized people, I've learned, will not tolerate even the smallest aberrations.

"I won't be here next Thursday. I have to go to the doctor," I say when it is my turn to share. I point to the spot on my forehead above my left eyebrow.

"I'm sure you're fine," Dr. Levine says. She's applied a dark brown shadow straight through her eyebrows today so she looks like Frida Kahlo. "Stop creating distractions from the therapy."

I noticed the spot on my forehead last night after my shower. It had been brown before, a freckle, and now looked bigger and had changed to a burnt red color. I took a picture with my phone and sent it to my mother in a text that said: "call me."

"Have you taken down The List from your refrigerator?" Dr. Levine asks me.

I clamp my lips and stare at the clock. It used to be so easy to know what to avoid: tobacco, saturated fats, drinking a fifth of vodka a day. Now you can be killing yourself by sleeping with your cell phone in the room (brain tumor); using lipstick (parabens—cancer); shampoo (sulfites—cancer); eating rice (arsenic); deli meat (nitrates—cancer); poultry (salmonella); red meat (mad cow); vegan soy products (breast cancer); or from aluminum foil to wrap food (Alzheimer's, Parkinson); water from plastic bottles (toxins leaked in warm or cold weather—infertility, cancer); Ziploc bags, plastic in shower curtains, raincoats, food packaging (phthalates—reproductive abnormalities, cancer). It was the plastics that were going to kill us all, apparently, and the planet too.

No one in my group or at my workplace is disturbed by these things. Not even my mother, who worries about, of all things, aliens landing on Earth and breaking into her house. "They'd come all the way to Earth in possession of the most highly advanced spacecraft ever known and care about your photo albums?" I asked her. "Your plasma TV?"

The fact that no one else is bothered by the avalanche of threats that come across their Facebook feeds makes me feel highly anxious. "Maybe it's prescience—a personal warning from the universe," I said to Dr. Levine when I first started the group even though I don't believe in *the universe* the way people like Annie and Dr. Levine do. "Maybe I'm worried about these things because one of them is actually going to kill me, specifically."

"The List is a fetish," Dr. Levine said. "When you process what happened in the park, you won't need to keep The List anymore."

"I want you to take that list off the wall and burn it when you get home," Dr. Levine says before we end the group that day. "Now, let's talk about the *park*."

I bristle. I am supposed to be in this group to talk about the fact that after being the prototypical, irritatingly dependable, studious type A up for a promotion to head of circulation for the Lewis College Library, I called my office mate, Sven, a cunt.

Dr. Levine had brushed past this incident in session one. "So you called someone a cunt," Dr. Levine said. She said this as if she were bored. As if I had sneezed in a meeting, not expelled an expletive that cost me a promotion and made my colleagues look at me like I was a serial killer.

"We would normally terminate you for this," my boss, Roxanne, informed me after the committee meeting the library board humiliatingly held to discuss the matter. "But your work is exemplary and this was entirely out of character. So, go to therapy for six months, and we'll decide then about long-term plans."

A woman in human resources handed me Dr. Levine's card. For days, my skin burned as if fire ants crawled up my dress.

Dr. Levine only wanted to talk about the park. She said once you experience trauma, your brain wires become crossed. You are no longer a trustworthy person to captain your own life. She said her patients needed to surrender to the therapeutic process completely.

"You need to let me tell you what to eat, what time to go to bed, and whom to speak to if you want to get better," Dr. Levine had said.

"Like in a cult," I replied.

By the next day, the spot on my forehead has raised a fraction of an inch, like a tiny loaf of baked bread.

"No one in our family has any face tumors," my mother says when I call. "Any news about when you can get your job back?" I can't concentrate on how annoyed I am at her lack of comprehension of my situation or the fact that I didn't lose my job—I lost a promotion—but I can't explain any of this because I have become paranoid that Dr. Levine will check my call history and know that I called my mother three times this week. I think about getting a disposable phone, the kind criminals use and throw away after they kidnap someone. I don't hear my mother's next few sentences. Only the last thing she says: "Remember Aunt Linda—your career is the most important thing you have as a woman."

On Thursday, I am in a gown on Dr. Havershore's dermatology exam table. He peers at the swatch of skin above my eye with a round magnifying device, like the kind jewelers use to assess the quality of a diamond. I can feel his breath near my face, steady as a radiator. He drops the magnifier into his lab coat pocket. "It's a basal cell," he says. "The surgeon will confirm, but I'm 99 percent sure."

"Cancer?" My mouth goes dry as concrete.

"Yes, but a very treatable kind."

"It's not even real cancer," Dr. Levine says when I tell the group my surgery is scheduled for the following week.

"They're going to cut into my face with a scalpel," I say. "So, I imagine it'll feel pretty fucking real." I'd received an email from the surgeon the night before. The Mohs procedure he would perform involved rounds of removing the infected flesh until the lab confirmed only healthy tissue remained. Dr. Levine makes a grunt somewhere deep in her throat and asks me to be sure not to schedule the surgery on the day of a therapy group session.

At home that night, I microwave a frozen organic meal. Enchiladas in green chili sauce. Cilantro diffuses into the room. I donated my previous microwave to the Salvation Army after reading somewhere that microwaves are carcinogenic. Or maybe it was that they rob food of all nutrients, which then makes you susceptible to cancer. Then I bought a used microwave from the same Salvation Army when I started Dr. Levine's group and lost my will to do basically anything once I got home. Dr. Levine says the extreme and flattening fatigue is due to my suppression of the trauma (*You'll get much worse before you get better*), but I think Dr. Levine is a vampire queen that feeds on her patients' neurons.

"You talk like a cancer patient," Dr. Levine said when I complained about my teeth-numbing tiredness to the group. "Patients feel fine with the cancer and think the chemotherapy is what's killing them. When the chemo is the only thing that's going to keep them alive." Right as she said this, my phone pinged with an alert that another $300 had been auto-deducted from my checking account. To: Dr. Elaine Levine.

Even with the portion of therapy my insurance covers, there will be no vacation this year, no restaurant meals, no new clothes. First-world problems, of course. I think of people in virtually every other country in the world, including my own, who do not get to eat enough every day. I am a privileged, selfish bitch. Knowing this does nothing to ameliorate my distress.

I stab my fork into the flesh of the tortilla. I would have liked another opinion—if there were anyone in my apartment to talk to. I had a boyfriend, Brian. We'd discussed getting an apartment together in Lakeview. Met with a realtor, went out to lunch at Summer House. We'd ordered oysters and talked about paint colors for the bedroom. Two weeks after we apartment shopped, he was text-fucking a girl he met online from California. "Our relationship is too predictable," he texted me later. I wished Brian had still been around—he would have enjoyed the cunt story.

The enchilada has not thawed all the way. I spit a chunk of frozen chicken in the trash and put the tray back into the microwave. The plate spins under a yellow light. I lift my eyes to The List smiling there on the blue piece of paper held to the refrigerator by a star magnet. Fuck Dr. Levine. Cancer is everywhere, including on my own face. My right hand shakes like a junkie. I finger the thin blue Bic pen in my pocket and imagine writing basal cell carcinoma in looping cursive along the open space midway down the page. "A compulsive wave lasts less than three minutes," Dr. Levine told the group. She makes us all pay five dollars to download the phone app that shows a multi-striped hot air balloon inflating and deflating at the rate we are supposed to breathe to help us ride out our compulsive urges.

It takes Dr. Patel five rounds to remove the basal cell. As he scrapes my epidermis, I imagine the balloon app is in front of my face and count my breaths: four, four, four, four. This works until Dr. Patel holds an instrument the size of a dental drill to my forehead. My organs start to shake. It takes my brain a minute to recognize the cauterizing pen. Understanding dawns in the brief but unmistakable smell of my own burning flesh.

Dr. Havershore sends me to Dr. Liss in plastic surgery for stitches.

"Wow, that's deep," Dr. Liss says as he stares at my face under a giant magnifying lamp.

"At least it's not serious," I say. I can't warm up after being in the cotton operating gown for five hours. My legs begin to shake again. The charcoal smell is stuck high up in my nose.

"I wouldn't say that," Dr. Liss says. "We saw a man a few months ago who didn't come in as soon as you did. Had to take out his whole eyeball."

My body sways like a tree. I grab the sides of the exam table.

"If you don't take care of something like this early, it'll go all the way to your brain."

It's dark when I leave the medical complex. I call an Uber, take the elevator to my apartment, and drop my bag inside the door. Without removing my coat, I walk to the refrigerator, take out the red Bic pen—all gleaming plastic filled up like a thermometer—and write "basal cell carcinoma" at the bottom of The List.

"Tell us about the park," Dr. Levine repeats over and over, like an AI version of a therapist. Dr. Levine was one of the pioneers of modern exposure therapy. A patient must relive and confront the trauma enough times that it loses its power. If the stories can be believed,

UNENDING DAY

Dr. Levine had once made a patient who had a phobia about deli meat cover his body with ovals of thinly cut smoked turkey. All the way up over even his face, like he was being buried in nitrates. I squish my eyes together, thinking that at some point, Dr. Levine will have the whole group tromp over to the park and lie down on the path exactly where it happened.

What happened is that one Thursday six months ago, I decided to walk home from the library instead of taking the 156 LaSalle bus. I like the way the park rolls from garden to nature museum to the Lincoln Park Zoo. The restaurants on the inner drive have fairy lights strung through them so all year long it looks like Christmas. Then I had to pee. I left the flare of the streetlights for the blue-black twilight on the bike path, where I remembered there was a public toilet. A bald bulb gleamed down over a doorway enough so I could see the women's restroom sign.

The man came from behind. Yanked my shirt collar so hard my eyes bulged. He pulled me to the last stall, where the light was burned out. He held me against the brick with his right hand across my mouth and began moving up and down the inside of my leg. I couldn't feel anything other than a cool numbness and the friction on my jeans. Couldn't tell if he had a gun or a knife. He was chewing cinnamon gum. The peppery smell stung my eyes. A minute later, three minutes—I have no idea, not long—he ran off toward the lion cages.

I kept telling Dr. Levine I appreciated how lucky I was. How I didn't need to be in the group. It wasn't a big deal when you think about it. No knife wound, no blow to the head, no gun pointed at my temple, no rape. Just a dog humping and a smell of cinnamon that would not fade. It was amazing how many foods contain cinnamon. Doughnuts, pumpkin pie, butternut squash soup, raisin bagels, tikka masala, sugar cookies, the sleepy time tea I used to drink at bedtime. I can't even stand in line at Starbucks anymore. Can smell the cinnamon in its clogged-up, perforated silver top all the way from the register.

"Say I destroy The List?" I say the next Tuesday in group.

"Did you?"

"No. But say I do. Am I finished? I'm healed?"

"You don't get over trauma," Dr. Levine says, and the rest of the group nod in a way that makes me want to punch each with my bare knuckles one by one. "You learn to live with it. You work on it the rest of your life."

I don't listen to the rest of the session. I watch the mold blooming on the limestone under the Macy's clock. I take the bus home and before Fullerton, I start seeing rings around the other people on the bus. I've heard people say they can see auras, beautiful colored fields of light like angel halos. I see spots of light. Sunbursts. I remember seeing this kind of impaired vision as a symptom of something. Looking up medical symptoms online is off-limits in Dr. Levine's treatment protocol. *Call a member of the group instead*, she told me the first week. I open a new browser on my phone and type in "halo spots, vision." I learn that I likely have a tumor on my optic nerve.

"I'm sure it's not an optic tumor." My mother's voice is thin with worry through the phone.

"Probably frontal cortex or in the cornea," I say.

"When is your progress meeting at the library?" my mother asks.

"Six months, Mom," I say. "They don't do early parole for good behavior."

"You were valedictorian of your high school, graduated with honors from the University of Chicago. Lewis College recruited you," my mother says. "You would have had the salary increase by now. The new office. You've not missed a day of work in two years. Surely they can see past one little . . ."

"I called someone a cunt, Mom."

One o'clock a.m. A motorcycle roars under my bedroom window. I pull a blanket from my bed to the couch in the living room. I wasn't even asleep. I sit on the worn cushion and think how I had been as shocked as Sven was to discover I'd called him a cunt. Yes, he annoyed me; no human adult with such wide shoulders and striking bald head should eat such tiny things so loudly. Baby carrots, one by one, from a plastic bag every afternoon. Big Gulp cups full of ice chips. Wasabi peas plucked by chopstick one by one from a can. I don't even remember calling him that.

"Cunt," the man in the park had said to me as he pulled his sticky leg off my jeans.

I smack the couch pillow into my face. The memory scampers like a squirrel. *Call me if you ever think about harming yourself*, Dr. Levine says practically every time she ends a group session.

The orchid I bought to invite a sense of life to the living room has stopped flowering. I make chamomile tea, but before it finishes steeping, I pour it down the sink. I check with the light of my phone. The box lists one ingredient: chamomile. But I smell it. Somehow there is cinnamon in that teabag—spicy and enough to cause a sneeze. I throw away the box. I can now add insomnia to my personal cadre of maladies. An Instagram post reports that deficient sleep can cut seven years off your life. I add "Insomnia" to The List.

I dig through the bookcase next to the couch to find the TV remote. Dr. Levine told me not to stream TV shows on the computer where social media posts and news headlines about diseases pop up like comic book bubbles every several seconds. I click up into the 300s on cable. A show about cats. Ghost hunters. Teen millionaires. I pause for a few seconds on a documentary about psychedelics. A group of veterans who'd served in Afghanistan stands in the rainforest sweating and vomiting, talking about being freed from PTSD. I envy those men molting their trauma off in the jungle while I am stuck with Dr. Levine's exposure talk therapy that goes on and on in a loop as endless as a barber shop pole. "Nature is the ultimate healer," one of the veterans on the TV says. He has a leg missing and a chunk of shrapnel emptied out half of his cheek.

I imagine myself in Peru or Mexico, drinking sunny leaves from an earthen cup. I'd go tomorrow, but hallucinogens won't cure me. I know it as much as I know Dr. Levine won't cure me. I stab at the remote buttons. Somewhere in the 350s, the ridges of a giant glacier plummet into a frothing blue ocean. I pull the blanket up higher over my hips.

The screen cuts to a man with cropped hair, a microphone in his hand. The background is a stunning summer vista. A soft valley with blooming wildflowers waving in front of a lake. Mountains rise behind with snow cascading down their peaks.

"Alaska is approaching its longest day. For the next two months, peaking with the summer solstice, Alaskans will experience near twenty-four-hour daylight."

The reporter speaks to a local family with four children, a couple who'd come to Alaska to experience the Unending Days on their honeymoon, an MD from Juno, who the reporter asked about odd behaviors he sees during the summer months.

"Most people handle it okay," the doctor says. "We see an increase in libido—lots of sunlight babies will be born in March. Some anxiety, fatigue. Some people are more affected than others. We had one woman here as a tourist last year—she broke up with her boyfriend by text, sold her condo in New York online, burned her clothes, and walked naked to a sporting goods store. Said she was *starting over*."

The doctor moves on to a list of prophylactic measures one can take to combat negative effects of the midnight sun: sleep masks, heavy curtains, drinking two liters of water a day. I want to hear from the naked woman. Is she happy she left her old life behind? Did she go back to the boyfriend, or did she still live in Alaska? Did she return to wearing clothes? I want to know what the woman had discovered in the shadeless day that altered her so dramatically. The reporter moves on to an interview with a man in a beige vest with many pockets who talks about bear hunting.

My temples throb. I open the meditation app. The striped balloon expands and contracts behind the whirr of a blue propane flame flickering against the digital cumulus clouds. I dream of a black glacier baking under an endless fiery eye.

Dr. Levine introduces a new group member on Tuesday. His name is Gerald. He has short gray hair and he wears pale blue Crocs. I wonder if he's a nurse or a doctor, but none of us find that out (what you *do* in the world is irrelevant here, according to Dr. Levine). Gerald confesses that a few months ago, he'd begun hiring women from Craigslist to come to his apartment and bite him until he ejaculated.

"They never touch my penis," Gerald says. "So it really isn't so bad."

"It's my anniversary today," Annie announces. I'm surprised to hear Annie is married. I'd envisioned Annie in a cheap apartment near Roger's Park, rolling a cart to the grocery store because, at forty-five or however old she is, she already moves like an elderly person.

"Twenty years with the doc here," Annie says. Dr. Levine looks elated and proud. The Goldilocks curls on her head bounce. I swing my head around the circle. "Are you kidding?" I ask.

"Best twenty of my life," Annie says. She leans under her chair and retrieves a white box of grocery store cookies from a recycled bag. Most of the cookies have broken in transit, their colors dulled by the powdered sugar and sticky with the jelly filling in the center of the flower-shaped ones. Cinnamon assaults me from the box. I hold my breath and pass the cookies away quickly. Peabo shares that she's gone a week without being paid for sex. Instead, she masturbates to the fantasy of fucking two men who each pay her $30,000.

I can't stop staring at Annie. Two-thirds of her life, Annie has come into this bland white-walled room, sat in one of the black chairs, and eaten dinner from a Tupperware while she talked about her sad life with Dr. Levine. The tableau horrifies me.

"I'm facilitating a weekend retreat next month," Dr. Levine announces. "Up in Lake Forest. We'll do psychodrama role plays. Two process groups a day. It's like therapy camp." Annie and Gerald look excited. The minute Peabo finishes sharing, I put on my coat and jog to the waiting room before the group starts to hold hands and chant, "The work will set you free."

Dr. Levine follows me to the waiting room.

"I talked to your boss today," she said. "I told them you weren't progressing as quickly as I'd hoped. You are still in so much denial. You have to open up to me, to the other members of the group. You have to want to get better." Dr. Levine recommends I add her seven o'clock a.m., Monday through Friday therapy group and the upcoming therapy retreat. "Ask your parents to help you pay for it," Dr. Levine says.

"You don't want me to call them for support, but I can call to ask for money," I say.

"Do whatever you have to do for the treatment," Dr. Levine says.

UNENDING DAY

Tonight's dinner: vegetarian lasagna. Even so-called organic meat often contains hormones and antibiotics, which could give you ovarian cancer or Lupus. I read the lasagna label looking for chemicals. Sometimes, when I inhale, I am certain I can feel the first tendril of a tumor forming in the soft folds of my brain's right hemisphere.

Sven has permanently moved out of our shared office, so the room is quiet and dark, like a grizzly cave. I don't begrudge him. If he'd called me a cunt, I probably could have had him fired for sexual harassment. I dump my blazer on the back of the chair, return a few emails, open my browser, and type "twenty-four-hour sunlight."

I read that Alaska has three million lakes larger than twenty acres, forty active volcanoes, 175,000 moose, 100,000 glaciers (six hundred of which are so large or interesting that they have proper names), and twenty-three mountain peaks in the 13,000+ feet club, including Denali, North America's tallest peak, at 20,320 feet. At latitudes higher than eighty-eight degrees thirty-three minutes north, far above human settlements—nature puts on a show called the "astronomical polar night." I read that slowly but surely the earth's axial tilt is changing—and with it, the Arctic Circle. The boundary line that defines the Arctic Circle retreats by about forty-six to forty-nine feet (fourteen to fifteen meters) northward per year. Fairbanks is known as the "Land of the Midnight Sun." From April 22 to August 20, the sun never seems to set. One can wake up in the middle of the night to find the sun shining brightly, people out running and gardening and walking the dog.

There are solstice festivals in Anchorage. Whole cruises designed around the Unending Days. The cheapest one costs $4,000. I check my bank balance. "Two hundred dollars." I punch numbers into my calculator. Each month, after rent and therapy, I could save twenty dollars.

The next morning, my mother is on the phone. "Dr. Levine emailed me. She says you're not following her treatment plan. She says you need more therapy. If you don't add groups, she says you'll need to go into an in-patient program at a hospital. She has a friend who runs one in Scottsdale."

I tell my mother that Dr. Levine is padding her bank account.

"There's a woman who's been in the group for twenty years!" I say. "How can you not be better in twenty years?"

"I told her we'd pay whatever insurance won't cover," my mother says.

"Great, you have my bank account number."

"Dr. Levine suggested we pay her directly."

"See?" I say.

"You're not dating. You won't move back here. You're on probation at your job. You're a wilting plant," my mother says.

I hold the phone a little away from my ear and worry about how much radiation I'm exposed to by holding this thing up against my cochlea.

"I want my daughter back."

I ask my mother: Does she want me to be eight again, reading *Island of the Blue Dolphins*? Or does she want twenty-something me? Graduating from the University of Chicago, straight into my master's at Madison, a predictable and trustworthy career path in front of me.

"Humans can never go back, Mom," I say. "Only forward, like airplanes."

"Call me every day at seven," my mother says. "Tell me you're okay."

When I wake up on Saturday, there are two messages from Dr. Levine: "We need to talk about adding the Monday–Friday sessions. And I need your registration for the weekend workshop."

Next message: "Friendly reminder: your treatment needs to be your number one priority."

I stand numbly in the bathroom. I can see my future, months turning into years. Nature hikes with the therapy group, weekend psychodrama workshops, eating dinner from the microwave. Barely an adult, a life of supervised activity in the name of mental health recovery. I stand in the kitchen, not remembering having walked there from the bathroom. I've bitten the inside of my cheek. I stick my index finger back near my molars. Blood highlights the rim of my fingernail. I fear this future the way some women fear dying alone in an apartment with a coven of cats.

That night, I eat raw vegetables that I wash in purified water and watch a 2018 documentary about Nuka, Alaska, called *The Stars Are Vanishing*. One speaker says that the oral tradition on which his culture teaches language requires new generations to see the stars clearly but because of light pollution from nearby cities, they can no longer see and the language is dying. Everyone I know—myself, Dr. Levine, Raquel, my mother, Sven—is all part of the problem. I switch off every light in my apartment and shroud my laptop screen with my duvet until I emit no light.

At work on Monday, my mother calls.

"Dr. Levine says you have still not signed up for the new groups. We sent the check. Your father and I are very concerned."

On Thursday an envelope arrives in the silver mailbox in my lobby. It's a plain business-sized white envelope with a sticker bearing my parents' home address in Michigan enclosed in a square of gold foil trim. Inside, a check. The memo says "therapy," but the check is addressed to me. Three thousand dollars. I feel a rushing sensation around my ears.

Three thousand dollars from my mother's personal Northern Pass savings account. I run my hand over the illustration of the ice-capped mountains. It's as if my mother is urging me forward. Giving me a sign.

Friday morning. Dr. Levine is sitting in my boss Roxanne's office when I get to the fourth floor. I clutch the rolled-up poster of the Denali glacier in my left hand. I reach for the library phone to call security when I remember again the waiver I signed, giving Dr. Levine permission to use "whatever means necessary" for my treatment.

"I've set up a new accountability structure with Roxanne," Dr. Levine says as if I am a junior high school athlete attempting to play in this week's game. "You'll fill out this online form," Dr. Levine says and gestures to an open laptop, "each time you attend your scheduled group. I've added the Monday–Friday meetings here as well, as you'll be starting those."

"This is unnecessary," I say to Roxanne. "I've made every agreed-upon session. Has my work suffered?"

"Dr. Levine said the symptoms may be hard to see," Roxanne says. Her large chest pushes the front of her striped shirt out over the lip of her desk.

"I explained to Roxanne that you're high functioning but deeply wounded. Anti-social. Dissociated. A very sick young woman," Dr. Levine says.

A knock comes at the door. I recognize the human resources director who held me in her office after the cunt event. Dr. Levine waves and smiles at the woman as if they are old sorority sisters about to go grab lunch.

"I'll see you this evening for group," Dr. Levine says and stands. "Please tell your mother I'll be calling her today to follow up about her check."

I tell Roxanne I have the check and want to deposit it immediately so I can pay Dr. Levine. I pass my bank and go to the credit union on La Salle. How many times have I walked past this place? Bulletproof windows and lottery posters lining the walls. Inside, it smells of charcoal and pine-scented air freshener. I'm seventh in line, behind a man in a stained army parka and battered work boots. I lean on my left foot, then right. A prickle runs up my neck and I spin, imagining Dr. Levine has followed me. I switch my phone to airplane mode. Then consider throwing it in the street, where it will be run over by a truck. It would not surprise me if Dr. Levine hacked into Apple and authorized herself with a "find my device" to all her patients' phones.

By seven o'clock I could be at O'Hare airport, leaving on the 8:00 p.m. to Vancouver. I think of the itinerary I have stuck to my refrigerator. The List has been removed without ceremony. I won't give Dr. Levine the satisfaction of knowing it's gone. If I share about Alaska, the group will lick its bones clean like piranhas.

I will have $3,000, and it only costs $1,500 in the off-season to board the cruise ship called *Shimmer Sea*. I could walk across the gleaming ramp, squinting in the sun and with the fatigue of having been awake for thirty-six hours. My eyes are electric and jittery, like I'm high, but I've only had water to drink. The hours melt into each other. I stand on the starboard side of the upper deck and spread my fingers over the dark oak railing.

Extraordinary sights. The white-tipped mountain, green valleys. A grassy bank out of which totem poles poke at the sky. The wooden eyes of carved falcons fall and hover on my face.

Sharp shadows appear under the deck chairs as the boat presses forward. The sun stays impossibly high, for hours upon hours. I fill myself greedily with the light, the infinity of it all. A guide in a blue vest walks around the deck, giving environmental details. "Alaska is made up of rainforests," he says. I hadn't read this. "Yep," he says. "You can hike through one in Tongass. Sitka blacktail deer, brown bears, feisty salmon." I'm about to ask him what makes the salmon feisty when he tells another couple that the tour will end as planned at the Land of the Midnight Sun Festival in Fairbanks.

GHOST HOUSE

I'd pictured only the glacial fields, the preening snow-covered peaks. I can see it, though, the rainforest he described. Heavy and green with hanging hemlock and old-growth spruce. Waves spray the stern of the ship. A bald eagle dives overhead. Children run past her on the way to the foosball table or the game room with its rows of video game consoles in the belly of the ship. I strip my jacket, then sweater. I don't apply sunscreen. Still the sun presses on us. I lift my neck to the face of the approaching mountain that stands guard over these waters. Light pours through my eyelids even when I squeeze them shut. When the deck clears for a minute, I open my throat and scream, as if I am one of the birds in the sky. An older couple hurries to the opposite side of the ship. The sky birds start to replace the megaphone voice of Dr. Levine. With every rise and dip of the boat I begin to empty out library consoles, cell phones, Sven, cinnamon, and footsteps running against pavement in the dark. Here, amid the towering ice caps, there is no space for these things.

The man in front of me at the credit union coughs and shuffles to the window. But I'm not really there. I'm on the boat. A wave lifts and drops us. A change in course. Northwest, someone says. Then, I see it. Even here in the middle of summer. A vertical glacier, a colossal wall of ice.

We sail past and gape. Nothing behaves as it should here. The sun does not set. Gravity cannot level the wall. The sun burns down on the snow demanding it melt. The ocean spits up waves, but the glacier wall refuses to cower. It seems to rise up higher as we draw close, stretching ever taller, solid, powerful, vast. Stronger for the fight.

NOT MY BODY

Yet, I am captive in my liberation.
Semen crystalized like a coral reef, inside.
Hands holding, Others' desires laid claim,
Rugburns appear like a spell on my thighs.
Religion too.
Easter morning, a bonfire
Treading with candles in dark hallways,
Prayers, not my prayers
Chants, not my chants
Magic, not my magic

Yet.

Hysterical
Emotional
Echoed aftershocks I feel now in my feet
All the way back to the paddles placed
On my grandmother's temples,
The wooden stick slid between her lips
Straps at her wrists,
Body jolts,
I jolt too, inside
where I am still a seed.

ACKNOWLEDGMENTS

As a friend of mine says, writing is a team sport. Tremendous thanks to the team at Muse: Patricia Fors, Gordon McClellan, Dominique Swanquist, Megan Jackson, Alexis Reyes and Alex Kuisis. Deep gratitude to Stuart Dybek and Juan Martinez for their invaluable mentorship at Northwestern- you made me the writer I am. Also to my writing coven: Auybn Keefe, Allison Epstein, Bridget Roche, Erika Carey. Thanks to the incredible women in Thought Leader Academy and Oracle- you are the SHERO's. And at the center of my heart: Bill, Finn & Maverick.

ABOUT THE AUTHOR

Sara Connell has been featured on The Oprah Winfrey Show, Good Morning America, The View, Fox, Katie Couric, and TEDx. Her writing has been featured in: the New York Times, Forbes, TriQuarterly, Good Housekeeping, and Parenting. She has presented at the Chicago Tribune Printer's Row Literary Festival, Northwestern University, Story Studio Chicago, Chicago Literary Alliance, and Chicago Women in Publishing as well as many Fortune 1000 companies: Estee Lauder, Johnson & Johnson, GE, Unilever. Her memoir Bringing In Finn was nominated for ELLE magazine Book of the Year.

Note on previously published stories:
"Marionettes" was published New American Legends, *https://newamericanlegends.com/2020/07/31/marionettes-by-sara-connell/*
An earlier version of "Tarifa" was published in I.O. *Literary Journal, https://www.ioliteraryjournal.com/*